Scandals In The Sanctuary:

The Beginning of a Series

S.C. Hill

Dreamer's
Vision
PUBLICATIONS

©2016 by SC Hill

Front Cover Design: Jonathan Snorten

ISBN: 978-0-9982486-0-8

Printed in the United States

Published by Dreamer's Vision Publications
Nashville, TN
dreamersvisionpub.com

Dedication

This is book is dedicated to my wonderful husband, James, who has been my biggest supporter and motivator. Thank you for all that you do! To my three beautiful children Malaysia, Major, and Micah I love you to the moon and back.

Table of Contents

Scandals in the Sanctuary:
The Beginning of a Series

Sunday Service Aftermath

Bishop Eugene Goodwin sat at his desk with his head down and rubbed his temples. He is exhausted and has a terrible headache. What he likes to call the Sunday service aftermath. He is the pastor of a rapidly growing church named Kingdom Life Ministries. He and his wife, Valerie, have been in ministry for many years but he has only been pastoring at Kingdom Life Ministries for five years. When he and his wife first founded Kingdom Life Ministries, they only began with eight members and held services in a high school gym. However, that didn't last long. The Goodwins hit the streets to bring the church to the people. They would have services at parks, nursing homes, hospital rooms, dorms and they even walked through the inner city, to witness and minister to those who were willing to receive. This way of evangelizing grew them out of the temporary gym site and into a 14000 square feet permanent building. Which currently houses about 300 members from all walks of life: old, young, rich, poor, black, white, and so on. Bishop Goodwin's main philosophy is to change many people's lives as possible with love and truth. He loves on everyone regardless of their mishaps, flaws, or social status. Sometimes his love can be tough love being that he's a "tell like it is" type of person. He speaks the truth, whether you want to hear it or not. But he always makes sure that he does it out of love. Bishop Goodwin raised his head as he heard the clacking sound of high heels coming towards his office. He knew it was his wife by the rhythm and pace. He welcomed his wife with a warm smile as she opened the door and entered. Every time he sees his wife, his face lights up even after 20 years of marriage. Wow! My wife is beautiful. *Lord, I thank Ya.* He thought to himself as he admired his well put together wife. She has on a gold dress suit that was very modest but still hugs her curves along with matching gold pumps. Her hair is in a curled wave-like layered bob. She barely wears makeup but she has on a berry colored lipstick that compliments her light brown skin. Valerie returned her husband's smile. He stood up and motioned for her to come closer. "Hey, honey. How are you feeling?" she said as she gave him a hug. He kissed her forehead, exhaled, and then shook his head. "So I am assuming Sunday service aftermath is on ten today?" she asked. "More like 100. I am so drained," he responded. "I bet! Service was amazing from start to finish. The praise team really did an awesome job, and the message you delivered has me so full.

And let's not forget two baptisms and three new members! God is so good!" Valerie said, thinking back on the wonderful service. "Yes, God is Good. God is good," he said repeatedly as he sat down at his desk with tears forming in his eyes. Valerie stood behind him and rubbed his shoulders. "There has been so many times when I just wanted to walk away from this. Church and ministry. Especially lately with everything that has been going on here. Sometimes I feel like no one out there understands the criticism, rejection, betrayal, loneliness, weariness, and frustrations that pastors go through. What happened in that service today is why I still continue on." He covered his face with his hands. Valerie stopped rubbing his shoulders and wrapped her arms around him and laid her head on his head. They were both silent for a few moments. During the silence, Lady Valerie thought about the times where she, too, wanted to quit the ministry. She felt as if her life was under a microscope. She had to watch what she say, do, go, dress and the list goes on and on. She, too, felt loneliness and frustration like her husband. Yes, she has a few friends and always surrounded by members of the church. Yet, she still feels lonely at times. She's married to her husband who is married to the church. So her constantly having to share him brings on frustration. She knows God has called him to do ministry, so she supports her husband fully, even if it means spending nights alone. Lady Valerie stood up straight and positioned herself beside her husband who still had his face covered with his hands. "Eugene, honey... I remember a sermon you did a couple years ago," Lady Valerie began. Eugene uncovered his face and sat up straight to listen to his wife. "You titled the message 'New Level New Devil'. You explained that as one grows in their walk with Christ, gets a promotion on their job, gets a breakthrough, is delivered, or whatever the increase may be, that a new devil stronger than the last one that was defeated will be waiting to intimidate you. But you said to not let that new devil hinder you from the next level. Our ministry is growing and you are helping impact so many lives. Of course the devil is going to attack. The enemy wants you to quit and give up on this ministry. But we know what God said. His promise is still good. Always remember that."

Eugene shook his head and smiled at his wife. "Thank you, love, I can always count on you to encourage the encourager." He took her hand and kissed it. There was a knock at Bishop Goodwin's office door. "Come in," Bishop Goodwin said aloud.

Deacon Alvin Roberts peeked his head inside. "Sorry, Bishop, to bother you, I know you are tired, but you are really needed in the sanctuary," he said with urgency. "What's going on?" he said as he hurried out of his office. "Just come quick!" Deacon Roberts said. As the two men headed to the sanctuary, Lady Valerie followed behind. She was stopped midway by Tara, Bishop Goodwin's administrative assistant. "Lady Valerie, I really need to talk to you," Tara said with a worried look on her face. "Are you okay?" Lady Valerie asked. Before Tara could answer, a loud commotion came from the sanctuary. "Dear God!" Lady Valerie shrieked with her hands over her heart. "Tara, we will talk in a moment." Lady Valerie promised and then rushed to the sanctuary to see what was going on. "But First Lady, I need to talk to you now," Tara said to herself as tears rolled down her face. A member saw Tara and grabbed her hand. "Come on, we have to get to the sanctuary," the member said. "Why?" Tara asked. The member responded, "Just another day at Kingdom Life Ministries."

No Weapons Formed

Chapter 1

Ratatatatata!!! Bang!!! Bang!!! Cack cack cack cack cack!!! The sounds of many guns being fired at once echoed through the night air. A few cars drove away from the area recklessly in different directions. Several people came out of their homes to see what was going on. "Omigod! Someone has been shot!" a woman screamed. "Someone call for help!" an older man yelled as he walked up to the body lying in the middle of the street. "An ambulance is on the way!" another woman yelled. The older man kneeled down near the body and discovered that the young man lying there had been shot several times. The young man managed to gurgle "Help me" as he coughed up a mouthful of blood. "Young brother, try not to move. My name is Alvin and help is on the way," the older man let the young man know. The young man closed his eyes. "Stay with us, brother! Open your eyes," Alvin continued to talk to the young man. The young man opened his eyes and gurgled through blood, "Don't let me die." "You are not going to die!" Alvin told him as he began to pray. "Jesus! I call on Your name! Father God, I am asking for Your grace and mercy on this young man. I don't know what transpired for him to be lying here, but I know You can raise him up! Do Your awesome works, Lord. I thank You in advance for his recovery. Thank You, Jesus! Amen." "Amen," a voice echoed. Alvin turned around to a woman standing nearby. "I believe that is Anita Davis' son," she told the man. "Anita Davis?" "Yes," the woman responded. "Do you know her?" she asked. "Yes. Yes, I do. We attend the same church," he told the woman. A few police cars and an ambulance pulled up to the scene. The paramedics rushed to the victim. The police officers began asking the bystanders what they heard or saw. All of them had the same story. No one saw anything; they just heard gunshots and cars speeding off. "Does anyone know the victim?" an officer asked. "I believe I know his mother," Alvin told the police officer. "But I do not know him," he continued. Another officer joined the first officer and the older man. "He may know the victim's mother," the officer told the second officer. "We retrieved the victim's driver license. His name is Joc Davis," the second officer informed them. "I am almost positive his mother is Anita Davis," Alvin told the cops. "Do you know where she may be?" one of the officers asked. "I didn't see her at bible study earlier tonight, I suppose she is at home," Alvin informed him. "Where are they taking him?"

Alvin asked. "County General," an officer answered. The victim was placed in an ambulance and rushed to the hospital. The officers continued to speak with the bystanders as the crime scene investigators retrieved evidence from the crime location.

Alvin rushed to his car where he left his cell phone. Once inside, he dialed his pastor. "Bishop! This is Alvin," Alvin immediately said once his pastor answered his phone. "Hello, Alvin! Is everything okay?" his pastor asked hearing the urgency in his voice. "Bishop, I need to get in contact with Sister Anita. Her son has been shot several times and has been taken to County General," Alvin informed his pastor. "My God! Sister Anita is still here at the church helping clean the sanctuary. I will tell her what has happened and take her to the hospital myself," the pastor told Alvin. "I will meet you there, Bishop," Alvin said before he ended the call.

Earlier that night, Joc Davis, also known as J.D., was at a sports bar with his homeboy, Kincaid. They were enjoying a football game while having a few drinks. "Hello, fellas! Do you two want another round of drinks?" a waitress asked. "Yes, ma'am!" J.D. answered. Staring the waitress up and down admiring her body. "Also let me get a round of you, too," he said, licking his lips. The waitress smiled and said, "You are so funny!" "But I am so serious," J.D. told her. "I'll be back with your drinks." The waitress told J.D. before she left the table. "My goodness! She's fine," J.D. told his homeboy. "Yeah, she is!" Kincaid agreed. "Aye man, ain't that Lil' Cecil over there?" Kincaid directed J.D.'s attention to an acquaintance of theirs. "Yeah, that's him. Why is he with Baldo?" J.D asked. "Good question!" Kincaid responded. "Don't let him see you," J.D. told his homeboy. J.D and Kincaid have been down with each other since grade school. They grew up in the same neighborhood and their mothers are best friends. Not only do they consider each other brothers but they are business partners as well. As youngsters, they got caught up in the street life: selling drugs, gang activity, and robberies. These criminal activities have gotten both men a ton of street cred and respect in their neighborhood and surrounding areas; however, it has also gotten them both a lengthy rap sheet as well. Both men were in and out of juvenile detention and jail since they were thirteen years old. Now that they are older, they aren't as reckless as they used to be. They are not standing on the street corners catching sales, shooting at rival gang members, or robbing people for the fun of it. Instead, they have others doing their dirty work. They have workers moving their drugs and handling their disputes. To make their earnings seem legal, they invested some money into a music studio. Music has always been an outlet for J.D. to express himself. He is an awesome lyricist and plays several instruments. Kincaid, on the other, hand is great at making beats and developing artists. So investing in a music production company was a good move for the two.

J.D. and Kincaid made themselves less noticeable by moving to another table where it was darker. They watched Lil' Cecil and Baldo engage in a conversation and then shake hands. "Man, what is really good?" Kincaid asked without taking his eyes off Lil' Cecil and Baldo. "Dude can't be trusted! We gotta get him handled ASAP!" J.D. said, hitting his hand in his fist. "Just say the word and that lil' nigga is dead!" Kincaid said, pulling out his Glock.

Lil' Cecil is a worker for J.D. and Kincaid, and Baldo is affiliated with a rival set of the two. So to see Lil' Cecil and Baldo together has the two questioning Lil' Cecil's loyalty and intentions. The two watched Baldo pull an envelope out of his jacket pocket and hand it to Lil' Cecil. Lil' Cecil and Baldo gave each other dap and Baldo left the sports bar. "What you wanna do, bruh?" Kincaid asked J.D. "Let's keep cool. We are going to leave out the back door and wait for him outside. Scoop him up, then see what this nigga up to," J.D. told Kincaid. J.D. signaled for the waitress to come to their table. "We're ready for our check baby girl," J.D. informed the waitress. He paid for their drinks and left the waitress a generous tip. "Hey, baby girl, do us a favor and let us go out the back door." The waitress placed the tip in her blouse and led the guys to the exit in the back of the building. Once outside, they made their way to the parking lot and got in Kincaid's Mercedes-Benz G wagon. J.D. pulled out his cell phone and made a few calls to some of the members in his set. He told them to meet him at their meeting spot. "Aye, bruh, there he go," Kincaid said, peeping Lil' Cecil exiting the sports bar. "Pull up on him!" J.D. instructed. "Wassup, mane?" J.D. said out the window playing cool. "Aye, bruh!" Lil' Cecil said, not knowing that they knew of his meeting with Baldo. "What y'all about to get into?" Lil' Cecil asked them. "Shid, we about to go hit up the strip club," J.D. told him. "Come hit the spot up wit' us. I'll bring you back to your car later," Kincaid extended an invitation to Lil' Cecil. "Yeah, I am down!" Lil' Cecil said as he opened up the back door to the truck to get inside. Once Lil' Cecil got into the truck, Kincaid pulled off, but they were not heading to the strip club. They pulled up to an abandoned building. Most of their meetings take place here. Five men were standing outside the building wearing all black and ski masks holding SKS Rifles and Sawed-off shotguns. One of the men in black came up to the truck. "What the hell is going on?" Lil' Cecil asked, confused by what was happening. "Same thing we wanna know, bruh," J.D. said as he got out the truck. The man that walked up to the truck opened the door where Lil' Cecil was and grabbed him out. J.D. and Kincaid, along with all the men in black, entered the building. "Y'all bugging, dude!" Lil' Cecil said as he was pushed to sit down in a chair. "Mane, shut yo' hoe ass up!" Kincaid yelled. "I just wanna know what this is about," Lil' Cecil said as all the men in black pointed their guns at him. "You done messed up and bit the hands that feed you, my nigga!" J.D. began. "You just like these hoes out here, you ain't loyal," J.D. finished. "Whatchu mean? I am loyal! Where is this coming from?" Lil' Cecil questioned. "We seen you with Baldo! That nigga ain't down wit us. And because of this, we ain't down with you! Blow his head off, mane!" Kincaid said. "Wait… wait…wait. Let me explain!" Lil' Cecil pleaded. "Just hear me out, I owed that man a debt in the past. Our meeting was settling the debt." As Lil' Cecil was pleading his case, J.D received several text messages from a reliable source of screened shot text messages between Lil' Cecil and members of Baldo's set and pictures of Lil' Cecil partying with them. "Well, the streets are saying otherwise," J.D. said as he handed his phone to Kincaid so that he could view all the messages he had just received. "Take care of our light work, fellas," Kincaid instructed the five men in black. Kincaid and J.D. left the building before the men killed Lil' Cecil. J.D. and Kincaid drove away from the area and headed back to their hood. As they got out the truck, they noticed a black car with no lights on at the end of the block. "Man, get yo' heat ready." J.D. calmly instructed Kincaid. "Mane, I am about to start bussing," Kincaid said as he pulled out his Glock and aimed it at the black car. The car sped towards the two. J.D. and Kincaid started shooting at the vehicle and the occupants in the vehicle retaliated. J.D. and Kincaid took off, running behind houses. While running, the two ended up separating. J.D. peeked around the side of the house he was behind. The coast looked clear, so he came out to the front still aiming his pistol. This time, a silver vehicle sped near him and a gunman shot at him multiple times. J.D. fired shots back and tried to run once again but ended up collapsing on the ground.

Chapter 2

"Where is he? Where is my baby?" Anita said as she rushed into the emergency room lobby at County General. "Somebody tell me where he is!" she yelled at the registrar at the lobby desk. "Ma'am, I would like to help you, but I need you to calm down and tell me who you are looking for," the registrar said. "My son! His name is Joc Davis. Where is he? Take me to him now!" Anita demanded. "Ma'am, I don't have any information on a Joc Davis," the registrar informed Anita. "What? But I was told he was brought here. Check again!" Anita said, becoming more upset. "Sister Anita. Keep calm. We will find him, okay?" her pastor, Bishop Goodwin, assured her. "Hello, ma'am. I know you said you don't have any information on Joc Davis. Who can I speak with? Because we were told he was brought here," Bishop Goodwin asked the registrar. "Why was he brought here?" the registrar asked. "He was shot multiple times earlier tonight," Bishop Goodwin answered. "I am sorry, I can't give any information on victims of crime but we do have an officer who you can speak to here. His mother will need to identify herself before any information is given," the registrar informed Bishop Goodwin. She then instructed them to go down the hall to an office where an on-duty officer was working. Bishop Goodwin and Anita went down the hall to find the officer. When they located the officer, Bishop Goodwin told the officer that they were told that Anita's son was brought here. The officer asked for both of their identifications. Once they were properly identified and Anita was able to accurately answer a series of questions about her son, the officer was able to share information about him. "Well, Ms. Davis, as you know, your son was a victim of a shooting tonight. He is currently in surgery. I will take you to the waiting room. Once he is out of surgery, the doctor will give you an update on your son's status." The officer walked Anita and Bishop Goodwin to the waiting room. "Thank you, officer," Bishop Goodwin said, shaking the officer's hand. "How long do we have to wait? I need to know if my baby is okay!" Anita said, pacing back and forth wringing her hands. "I don't know, hopefully, we will hear something soon," Bishop Goodwin said, patting her on the back. "Bishop Goodwin, Sister Anita. How is he?" Deacon Alvin Roberts said, coming inside the waiting room. "He's in surgery. We don't know anything yet," Bishop Goodwin answered. "Deacon Roberts! Tell me everything you saw," Anita said, rushing to Alvin. "I didn't see what happened.

We found him after the incident. He was able to speak to me. I prayed for him and he squeezed my hand before they took him in the ambulance," Alvin told her. "I sent out a message to all the saints to pray for Joc and I want us to continue to pray for him as well. The Lord said, 'For where two or three are gathered together in my name, there I am in the midst of them.' And as we all know, where Jesus dwells, His glory is with him," Alvin continued. Bishop Goodwin nodded his head at Alvin's statement and then grabbed both Alvin's and Sister Anita's hands. "Let us pray. Heavenly Father, we call on you right now as we touch and agree and combine our faith in you. We know that you are all-powerful and we pray that you touch the surgeon's hands as he performs this surgery. Give him patience, compassion, and a clear focused mind as he puts everything back together. Bless the hands of everyone in that operating room working on his behalf from the surgeon to the nurse, on down to the surgical tech," Bishop Goodwin managed to say before a doctor came into the waiting room. "Ms. Davis? Sorry to interrupt. I am Dr. Zeliski. I was Joc's surgeon tonight." "How is he? Please tell me everything is okay!" Anita asked. "The surgery was successful. Luckily none of his main arteries or organs was pierced. He lost a lot of blood so he had a blood transfusion. However, all his vitals are good and he is resting. With time he will make a full recovery," Dr. Zeliski informed. "Praise God! Thank you, Jesus! Thank You, Lord!" Anita rejoiced through tears. "Hallelujah! Thank You, Father!" Bishop Goodwin joined in. "The prayers of the righteous availeth much! Glory God!" Deacon Robert's clapped his hands. "Can we see him?" Anita asked. "Yes. Follow me," Dr. Zeliski answered, and then took the three to J.D.'s room. Anita gasped at the sight of J.D. He had tubing in his nose, an I.V. drip, as well as being hooked to a heart monitor and blood pressure machine. Anita pulled up a chair next to J.D.'s bed. "Mama's here, baby," she whispered and grabbed his hand. "I will leave you all alone. If you need me, I will be right outside," Dr. Zeliski told them. "Thank you, Doctor." Anita acknowledged Dr. Zeliski. "God Bless you!" Bishop Goodwin said, shaking Dr. Zeliski's hand. Dr. Zelinski nodded his head and left the room.

"Joc," a still voice called. Joc looked around searching for who called him. He didn't see anyone. Everything was bright, so bright that he couldn't make out any shapes or colors. "Joc." He heard the still voice again. Joc tried to get up but couldn't move. He began to panic at his immobility. Then he got a whiff of a sweet fragrance that put him at ease. Joc felt a presence come near him and even though he couldn't see who it was, he felt safe. Images of being shot flashed in front of him, he felt himself lying on the ground in a puddle of blood, sirens blasting in his ear; he dozed off at the sight of an oxygen mask being placed over his nose and mouth. More images flashed in front of him from his childhood to his mother holding him as a baby. The images stopped and he was still surrounded by brightness. " Joc, my child. I love you so much. My thoughts and plans for you, are great and mighty. This life you have been living is not my plans for you. Seek me. I am all you need. I will restore you and set you free. Will you trust me?"

"Joc baby?" Anita said as she felt Joc squeeze her hand. The nurse on duty smiled as she finished taking Joc's vitals. "Call his name again and see, if he will respond," the nurse instructed. "Joc, I love you. Are you ready to wake up?" The excitement showed all over Sister Anita's face as Joc squeezed her hand again. Joc slowly opened his eyes and began to blink until his sight was adjusted on his mother's face. "He's awake!" Sister Anita said with a big smile on her face. "That's wonderful!" the nurse said. Joc yawned and glanced around the room. "Hi, Momma," he managed to say through coughs. "Why am I here?" he asked. "You were shot several times, but you're going to be okay," she said, rubbing his hand. "How long have I been here?" Joc asked, noticing all the balloons and flowers in his room. "A few days. You will be able to come home soon," she answered. "Joc baby, do you remember anything at all?" she questioned about that night. Joc closed his eyes to think back to that night. "I remember being with Kincaid and a car approaching us. We were running and—" Joc paused as he tried to sit up but was too pained to do so. "You're going to be pretty sore for a while. Try not to move too suddenly. Later, we will see if you have enough energy to stand up. Here, take this," the nurse said as she gave him pain medicine. "Thank you," Joc said, taking the medicine. "I will leave you two alone. Press the call button if you need me," the nurse said, and then exited the room. "Mom, is Kincaid alright? Where is he?" Joc asked, concerned about his friend. "He's fine. He has come up here several times checking on you. He was questioned by a couple of detectives about that night. He didn't have much information to give," Anita said, adjusting Joc's pillow behind him. "This is wild. Someone wants me dead! What am I suppose to do when I leave here? What if these niggas know where I lay my head?" Joc questioned. "I don't want you to worry about that. I just want you to get better. I believe you were at the wrong place at the wrong time," Anita said, trying to keep Joc calm. "I know you are starving! I am about to go see about the nurse bringing you some food," Anita said, continuing to shift the conversation. "Yes, please I am hungry. Hungry enough to eat hospital food!" he managed to let out a little laugh. "You're so silly, boy! I'll be right back." Anita shook her head and smiled. She left the room and closed the door behind her. She stood there for a moment and thought about what Joc said about someone wanting him dead. Worry and concern consumed her. She closed her eyes and tilted her head back, and then exhaled. "Lord, thank You for Your grace and mercy over my son's life. I just ask that You continue to keep Your shield of protection over him. No weapon form against him shall prosper. I pray that he finds solace in You and learns to love You as much as You love him. Lord, I thank You once again. Amen."

Chapter 3

A couple of weeks have passed since the night of the shooting. Joc has been out of the hospital a little over a week and has been staying with his Mom. "Hey, Mama! What you in here burning?" Joc said as he walked into the kitchen where his mom was finishing up cooking. "Hush! I am not in here burning nothing," she said, throwing a dish towel at him. "I hear ya," he said, dipping a spoon inside some banana pudding Anita just made. "Aye, get out of there! That's for the church picnic," she shooed him away from the dish. "Is the chicken and mac-n-cheese for the church, too?" he asked. "Yep!" "What about these green beans and potato salad?" "It's all going to the picnic," she informed him. "Dang! Are you the only one bringing food?" he questioned of the large quantity she prepared. "Boy, get out the way and leave me alone. I made you a couple of plates already," she said as she began to pack up all the food into bags. "Yeah! That's what I am talkin' bout. Thank ya!" Joc said, rubbing his hands together grinning. He walked to his Mom and gave her a kiss on the cheek. "You're welcome, baby! Now get out of my way because I am running late," she said as she placed utensils in another bag. "I'll take these out to the car for you," Joc said, grabbing all the bags. "Thank you, son, but you don't need to be carrying all that. I don't want you to have a setback. After all, you are still healing," she said. "Mama, it's all good. I am fine. I know my limits. Carrying a few bags of food will not have me on the floor in fetal position crying in pain," he said of her concern. "After all, check out these arms," he said, flexing his muscles, "these babies can lift anything." He flashed his mother a big smile. Anita shook her head. "You a mess, boy." Joc headed out to his mother's car. As he was putting the items inside, Kincaid pulled up the driveway and blew his horn. "Waddup, man?" Joc said, raising his hand. "Nothing much." Kincaid responded out the window. He got out of his vehicle and walked up to Joc. They shook hands and leaned in for a side hug. "Whatchu out here doing?" Kincaid asked. "Man, bruh just putting some stuff out here for Moms. She about to go to church." "Church? Today Saturday, though," Kincaid said, confused. "Church picnic. Besides, you know my Mama practically lives in that church," Joc informed. "Oh okay and yeah, she is always there," Kincaid said as he followed Joc inside of the house. They walked into the kitchen. "Hey, Mama Anita!" Kincaid greeted as he grabbed a biscuit off the counter.

"Aw shoot you in for it now," Joc whispered to Kincaid. "Kincaid, put that biscuit down! That's for the church picnic. You always coming in here eating," Anita fussed. Joc burst out laughing. "I told you, man!" "Is it like that? I can't have a biscuit? You hard on me," Kincaid laughed. "You can have all the biscuits you want," Anita told him. "See, I knew you loved me," Kincaid began to say before Anita interjected. "If you come to the church picnic!" she said, grabbing the basket of biscuits off the counter. "Got'emmm!" Joc yelled, and then started laughing out loud. "Really? It wasn't even that funny." Kincaid said at his friend's laughter. "It really was." "Shut up, fool." The two carried on. "Alright, boys, let's not act like children," Anita said of their lighthearted feud. "I am serious. You two should come to the picnic. Good people plus food, add in live music and games equal great fellowship," Anita invited. "I don't know about all that," Joc said, not feeling the invite. "Will there be some fine ladies there?" Kincaid asked, rubbing his hands together. "Yes! Fine wholesome ladies. No thots!" Sister Anita told him. "What you know about some thots? Besides, all churches have thots," Joc responded. "Yep! Them church girls be the biggest freaks!" Kincaid agreed. The two gave each other a high five and laughed. Sister Anita looked at them sideways and rolled her eyes. "Lord, help them! Because they need it," she said of their comments. "Well, I am out of here," Anita told the guys. Joc walked her out. "And don't be in my refrigerator, Kincaid," She said as she walked out the door. "Love you, Mama Anita!" Kincaid said in a sing-song voice. "Yo' Mama something else," Kincaid told Joc as they went inside the living room. "Who you tellin'?" Joc responded. "So what's up man? Is business still running smooth?" Joc asked being that he's been out of the loop of things. "Yeah, everything is running smooth. There has been bookings left and right at the studio. And the new connect has been coming through for us. As a matter of fact, this is for you," Kincaid informed him and handed him a large amount of cash in bands. "Them runners out there pushing!" Joc grinned referring to the workers who sell their drugs. "Hey, everybody trying to eat. Speaking of eating. Please tell me yo' Momma left a plate behind or something," Kincaid said, walking to the kitchen. "Yeah, she left me two plates. You can have one. I am about to put this money up and grab my stuff so we can roll out," Joc said, and then walked down the hallway to his room. Once inside his room, Joc pushed his dresser to the side and pulled up a floorboard. Under the floorboard was a stash of cash and his gun. He placed the money Kincaid just gave him inside and removed his gun. He placed the floorboard back down and pushed the dresser drawer back over it. Joc went to his closet and pulled out his bulletproof vest and put it on along with his holster. He concealed his weapon, and then put on a shirt and went back to the kitchen. "You ready to head out?" Joc asked Kincaid who was hunched over stuffing his face with food. Kincaid shook his head yes, while chewing. "Man, Mama Anita plays no games in the kitchen!" Kincaid said, licking his fingers. "Why you think I haven't gone back home yet? Shid, Mama feeding me too good," Joc said of his mother's good cooking skills. The two headed out and got in Kincaid's ride. "Where to, bruh?" Kincaid asked. "Let's just ride. I been laid up so long. I am just happy to be out the house," Joc said, leaning his seat back. "I feel ya," Kincaid said, handing Joc a joint. "Fire that up, man, I know you need one." "You know me all too well." Joc took the joint and in no time they both were lit. "Listen to this, bruh. I put together some beats for this chick name Sasha. She straight fire on this track," Kincaid said, playing the song. Joc nodded his head as he listened to the sultry voice singing on the smooth mellow hip hop beat. Joc began to snap his fingers and move his shoulders back and forth continuing to nod his head. "Yeah this dope, bruh! You did your thang on this one, and ole' girl got a voice on her." Joc gave Kincaid props. Kincaid was in his zone, so he just nodded his head at the compliment. Kincaid continued to drive when they passed Joc's mom's church. "Kingdom Life Ministries," Joc read the sign. For a moment he was memorized by the sign. He's seen the sign before in passing. But today it felt as if it was his first time seeing it. His Mother always beg him to come to church with her but he always decline. However, all of sudden he felt a pull on him to go. "I see why Mama Anita cooked so much food, it's slam packed over there," Kincaid said, passing by the church. "Aye, turn back around. Let's go check it out." Joc said, looking back at the church. Kincaid glanced over at Joc with a look of confusion. "For real, bruh?" "Yeah, turn around." Joc shook his head. "For what, though?" Kincaid questioned. Joc didn't want to explain the feeling that suddenly came over him, so he played it off as hunger being the reason. "Man, free food! What other reason, ninja?" Joc said, and then laughed. "I ain't that bold. I may be high but I still have sense enough not to take my high ass to that church," Kincaid brushed off the thought. "So you not hungry?" Joc asked. Kincaid burst out laughing. "Dude, I can't take you serious right now, but I am hungry, though." "Well let's go get a plate," Joc said coolly. Kincaid made a U-turn and headed to Kingdom Life Ministries. They managed to find a parking space, but was hesitant to get out the vehicle. "Man, I am too high for this! Lord, please know this was not my idea," Kincaid said out loud. Joc began to think about what Kincaid had been saying. Maybe this isn't a good idea. *I wouldn't want to embarrass Mama in front of all the church folks here,* Joc thought. Joc stared at the church sign and once again felt drawn to come inside. "Forget it, let's go in," Joc told Kincaid. Kincaid still had his reservations but went along with Joc. Signs for the picnic directed them to the side of the church. Before walking over both gentlemen straightened their posture, wiped down their clothes as if they were dusty, and sprayed chronic killer all over themselves to eliminate the odor of marijuana. "You cool?" Joc asked Kincaid. "Yeah, you cool?" Kincaid reciprocated. Joc shook his head yes. The churchyard was very live. Music and laughter filled the air. Children were running around playing tag and jumping in bouncy houses. Several men were on the grill talking about sports, while some men were playing flag football. There were ladies serving food and many ladies in huddles talking and laughing. Joc and Kincaid were greeted by many as they made their way over. They also encountered strange looks as well. "Joc? Kincaid?" they turned around to see Anita standing behind them surprised at their presence. "I can't believe you two decided to come," she said with a big smile, and then gave them both a hug. As she hugged them, she whispered to them, "Y'all didn't come looking for women, did you?" "No, ma'am" Joc responded. "Welllll," Kincaid said before laughing and telling Anita he was just kidding around. "Okay. Good. Well, let me introduce you to a few people," she said, grabbing them both by the hand. She introduced them to almost everybody including Bishop Goodwin. "Who do we have here?" Bishop Goodwin asked as Anita walked up with Joc and Kincaid. "This is my son, Joc, and his best friend, Kincaid," Anita informed. Bishop Goodwin extended his hand to shake Joc's and Kincaid's hand. "Joc and Kincaid, it's a pleasure to meet you both." "Joc, Bishop Goodwin prayed for you while you were in the hospital and he stayed with me until I knew you were alright," Anita informed Joc. "Thank you, sir, I really appreciate that!" Joc expressed his gratitude. "No need to thank me. I am just glad you are up and well." Bishop Goodwin responded. "Well, I am glad you two are here. I want you all to enjoy yourselves and I hope to see you both again soon." Bishop

Goodwin smiled and gave Joc a pat on the shoulder. Joc nodded his head and watched Bishop Goodwin and his mother walk away. "Hey, man, I am about to go take this call. I'll be back," Kincaid informed Joc. "Alright, man, I'll see you in a minute" Joc responded. "Joc?" a man approached Joc as if he knows him. Joc tried to place his face but couldn't. "Hi, I am Alvin Roberts." Alvin extended his hand to shake Joc's hand. "Hi. Have we met?" Joc asked returning the handshake. "Well, not officially until now," Alvin started before pausing. "I was there with you before the ambulance came, you are real trooper," Alvin finished. As Alvin was talking, images of that night came back to Joc's remembrance. Joc saw Alvin's face as he assured him he will be alright. "It's so good to see you," Joc heard Alvin say as he came back to reality. "I remember you praying for me and assuring me I wasn't going to die. Thank you, sir!" Joc said, shaking his head and swallowing back emotions that were beginning to rise. "You're welcome! I just did what any person with a heart would have done," Alvin said before giving Joc a brief hug. "Deacon Roberts, I see you've met my son," Anita joined the gentlemen. "Yes, I have. Joc, you have a great mom, we love us some Sister Anita around here," Deacon Roberts shared. Anita blushed at the comment. Joc noticed his mom blushing and stared at her. Anita made eye contact with Joc. Joc smiled, and then nodded his head towards Deacon Roberts, and then he raised his eyebrows at her to insinuate that she may have a little crush on Deacon Roberts. Anita shook her head no and mouthed the word "stop" to Joc. Joc laughed at his mom's gesture. "What's funny? I want to laugh," Deacon Roberts asked. "Don't mind him, Deacon, he's a nut," Anita said discreetly giving Joc the eye. Deacon let out a small laugh. "Well, Joc, I hope you will come visit us soon." "Yes, me, too, I've been trying to get him to come visit forever now," Anita said of the many failed attempts of getting Joc to church. "Hi, Dad! Hi Sister Anita!" a young woman came over and greeted. "Hey, sweetie!" Anita said, giving the young woman a hug. "Hi, pumpkin," Deacon Roberts greeted back as he kissed the young woman on the cheek. "Joc, this is my daughter, Tara; Tara, this is Sister Anita's son," Deacon Robert introduced the two. "Hi, Joc!" Tara smiled and extended her hand to shake his. "Hi, Tara, it's nice to meet you," Joc said, returning the smile and shaking her hand. "So what are you guys talking about over here?" Tara asked. "Well, we were just telling him we hope to see him at church soon," Deacon Roberts answered. "Yes, it would be awesome to have you,"

Tara said with a smile. "I'll definitely be here tomorrow," Joc informed. "Great!" Deacon Robert said with excitement. "Awesome!" Tara said just as excited as her father. "Well, we will see you tomorrow morning," Deacon Roberts said as he motioned for Tara to come with him to leave. "Have a good evening, Joc," Tara said, still smiling as she followed her father. Joc watched the two walk away. "Oh really?" he heard his mother say. Anita was standing with her arms crossed in front of her chest. Joc was ready for his mom to wear him out. "What's wrong, Ma?" "I've been trying to get your behind to come to church for years. And you always say no, but let a pretty young thang come in your face skinning and grinning, now you talkin' about I'll definitely be here tomorrow. Boy, you are something else," she said, shaking her head. "Well, if I knew you had ladies that look like Tara in there, I would have came a long time ago," he said, rubbing his hands together as he looked at some of the women at the picnic. "Don't you go after Tara, or any woman at this church for that matter. You hear me?" she scolded. "Momma, I am just kidding. I am coming because I have a lot to be thankful for." Touched by Joc's statement, she wrapped an arm around his waist and laid her head on his shoulder. "And for that, I am thankful."

Chapter 4

Joc found him a seat near the back of the sanctuary. He was a little late coming into service and didn't want to cause too much attention to himself. He came in at the tail end of praise and worship. He sat down and watched as everyone else was up on their feet singing and clapping along with the praise team. He nodded his head and occasionally tapped his foot to the high tempo song. He was fascinated by the energy of the saints. It reminded him of a party. However, this party was different from what he is used to. Instead of turning up in a club, they were getting turnt in the church. Instead of being drunk of alcohol, they were spiritually drunk. *They are too hype!* Joc thought to himself. At one point he laughed at how hard the saints were going in. He wasn't laughing at them because he thought they were funny, but he was laughing because he never witnessed anything like this. The atmosphere shifted to another level. The music stopped and no one was singing, all you could hear was feet stomping and hands clapping. It was thunderous. Joc felt chills. He could no longer sit down and watch he wanted to participate. He stood up and clapped his hands. The bass guitarist started to play a few runs, and then the drummer was right behind. Which created that praise break shout music sound. Folks took off running left and right. Saints were jumping, high-stepping, dancing, marching in place, shouting, still stomping and clapping and so on. Bishop Goodwin was now standing at the pulpit just smiling as he watched the saints erupt with praise. Every time Bishop Goodwin tried to speak, he would get a quickening in his spirit that he couldn't get his words out. "Yes, God! Hallelujah!" Bishop Goodwin managed to say. "The Lord is here, y'all unlocking some things in this place. If you're not tuned in, you better get tuned in because God is moving in here," Bishop Goodwin continued. "Yassssss!" Bishop Goodwin's wife, Lady Valerie, shouted while waving her hands in the air. Lady Valerie's shout caused Bishop Goodwin to break out in a praise dance. Which took the church to a higher level of praise. Bishop Goodwin attempted to begin his sermon again. He looked out at the congregation who were beginning to calm down. "If I didn't know any better, I would think y'all don't want me to preach today," Bishop Goodwin said with a big smile. "If I was one of them pastors that go strictly by the program, I would tell y'all to sit down and act like you got some sense so I can get this message out. But y'all know I ain't traditional and if the spirit is moving in this place, I am not stopping it," he said. "Amen, pastor!" a saint yelled. "But I do have a word for somebody before I try to get to my message," Bishop Goodwin began. He stepped down from the pulpit and began to walk down the aisles of the pews. "The Lord just told me to tell somebody here, to exchange your bullet proof vest for his armor. The armor of God. I don't know who I am talking to but he wants to restore you and free you." Bishop Goodwin said, looking around for who this word is for. Joc began to feel uneasy. Sweat beads formed on his forehead. *This is getting crazy*, he thought to himself as he touched his stomach to feel the bulletproof vest under his shirt. Everyone was still standing. He wanted to sit down but was afraid that would cause the pastor to notice him. Joc looked down at the floor to avoid eye contact with Bishop Goodwin who was now walking near the pew where he is. As Joc looked down, images of bright lights and a still voice came to his remembrance. He could only remember a small part but the words restore and free stood out to him. "He wants to free you from bondage. You can get that freedom today," Bishop Goodwin continued as he walked to the altar. Joc took a deep breath and made his way to the aisle. He walked to the altar, not knowing what exactly would happen once he got there. But he knew that the Lord was speaking to him and he had to move. Bishop Goodwin studied Joc as he stood at the altar. "Young man, this word is indeed for you. He wants you to switch your armor." Joc slowly rolled his shirt up his torso and over his shoulders to remove his shirt. Next, he removed his bulletproof vest exposing his bandages that covered his wounds. As he stood there he heard the familiar still voice again. "Trust me." Joc knew that this voice was God. Joc slammed his bulletproof vest on the altar and raised his hands in the air. With tears in his eyes, he yelled, "I trust you, God! I trust you!" His actions caused the church to erupt with praise. "Thank You, Lord! Hallelujah!" Anita shouted from her post at the door. "You want to live for Christ?" Bishop Goodwin asked "Yes, sir," Joc answered. "You ready to repent and be baptized." Bishop Goodwin continued. Joc shook his head yes. "Well, amen! Saints, we have a young man who wants to be baptized," Bishop Goodwin happily announced. Joc was taken back by an usher to get him ready for baptism. "See sometimes we can't go by the program! I love when God interrupts our plans. Because, as you all know, nine times out of ten our plans is not the Lord's anyway. He wants lives saved today, He wants folks freed today. That young man just threw his bulletproof vest down. I didn't know he had a vest on! That was nobody but God. Gloraaay!" Bishop Goodwin said before opening up the altar for those who were in need of prayer. The curtains to the baptism pool opened up in front of the sanctuary. Deacon Roberts was standing in the pool. He extended his hand to Joc to step down into the water. Joc stood sideways in front of Deacon Roberts with arms crossed over his chest. Bishop Goodwin instructed the congregation to extend their right hands towards Joc. Bishop Goodwin nodded at Deacon Roberts to go forth with the baptism. "In obedience to our Lord and Savior Jesus Christ, and upon your profession of faith, I baptize you, my brother, in the name of Jesus Christ for the remission of your sins, and ye shall receive the gift of the Holy Ghost. Amen." Deacon Roberts submerged Joc under the water and lifted him back up. Joc wiped the water from his face. And began to jump up and down shouting "Thank you, Jesus." Sister Anita, full of joy, took a victory lap around the sanctuary. The musicians began playing and the church sang 'I've been down in Jesus Name.' Shortly after, Joc returned to the sanctuary after drying off and changing back into his clothes. He returned to the altar and joined Kingdom Life Ministries.

His mother was elated. She embraced him with a big smile and eyes full of happy tears. "Thank you, Jesus! Thank you!"

***

"Oh yeah, that sounds good!" Bishop Goodwin said as he came into the sanctuary. The praise and worship team just got finished rehearsing for Sunday's service. It has been a few weeks since Joc joined Kingdom Life Ministries. He was welcomed with open arms and he already loves his new church family. Joc has practically been living at the church. He's there more than any other place. He comes to bible study, Friday night prayer, he gives piano and guitar lessons to some of the youth, he helps out around the church and he joined the music ministry where he plays the keyboard. After rehearsal, the musicians decided to freestyle a bit. Joc was playing a mellow tune on the keyboard that has a jazz sound. The guitarists, drummer, and saxophonist joined in. The praise team hyped them up to keep going. And for the musicians to see Bishop Goodwin jamming out, they decided to give a full show. Bishop Goodwin stood by the guitarists and played his imaginary guitar. He nodded his head in rhythm with the drummer and then shook his head and made a stank face at the smooth rich sound of the saxophone. The musicians were sounding so good he couldn't help but make an ugly face. "Yes! You better tickle them keys," Bishop Goodwin said as he stood by Joc as he continued to flow on the keyboard. The musicians wrapped up their little jam session. Then conversed among themselves before packing up their things and leaving. Joc stayed behind to talk to Bishop Goodwin who was now in his office. "Hey, Tara! How are you doing today?" Joc asked as he walked up to her desk. "Hi, Joc, I am great! How are you?" Tara reciprocated trying not to smile too hard. Joc was warned by his mother not to make any moves on Tara and so far he hasn't. But not without a struggle. Tara is a beautiful woman and the way she smiles at him does something to him. "Do you need to see Bishop?" she asked Joc. "Yeah, can you see if he will see me?" "Sure, one moment." She paged Bishop Goodwin. "Pastor?" she said on Bishop Goodwin intercom. "Yes, Tara?" Bishop Goodwin answered. "Brother Joc would like to speak to you. Can you see him now?" "Yes, let him in," Bishop Goodwin responded. "He's able to see you," Tara said as she got up from her desk. She walked to Bishop Goodwin's office door. Joc walked behind her as she led him. The way her hips swayed when she walked, Joc couldn't help but notice her assets. "You can go in," Tara said, opening the door. "Joc?" Tara said as she noticed Joc didn't move. "Huh?" Joc said, shaking out of his trance. He was so caught up on her best features that he didn't hear her. "You can go in now," she told him. "Right, Thanks!" he said, feeling a little embarrassed. She smiled at him once more and walked back to her desk. Joc entered Bishop Goodwin's office. Bishop Goodwin was putting a large amount of cash into a bank deposit bag. *Wow, that's a lot of paper!* Joc thought to himself as Bishop Goodwin put the bag of money in his filing cabinet and locked it. "So, Joc, you want to talk to me, what's on your mind?" Bishop Goodwin said, taking a seat at his desk and motioning for Joc to have a seat as well. Joc sat in one of the chairs in front of Bishop's desk. "Well, sir, I am kind of in a predicament that's hard to get out of," Joc started. "What kind of predicament?" Bishop Goodwin asked. Joc began to speak and then hesitated. In the last few weeks, Joc has literally turned in life around. He doesn't hang around his old environment that is full of trouble. He stopped drinking alcohol and smoking. He even told Kincaid he wanted out their street hustle. However, he is still a partner with Kincaid when it comes to their production studio. Lately, though, he has been thinking about giving that up, because it was bought with drug money. Joc truly wants to be legit now. One of the brothers at

Kingdom Life Ministries introduced Joc to a public relation manager who has helped Joc get speaking engagements. Joc has gone to high schools and after school programs sharing his story. He knows sharing his story may prevent a young boy from getting involved with gang activity and drugs. With a second chance at life and finding his purpose, putting it in jeopardy is no longer an option. Joc took a deep breath and finally spoke. "Bishop, I just want to right my wrongs. I have done some things I can't even speak on. I have been embedded into these streets so long that the only way out is to die out. They not just go let me walk away." Joc stood up and paced back and forth across Bishop Goodwin's office. "I don't want to live in fear. I have never valued my life or been afraid to die in these streets. But now I am afraid of losing my life because of my past!" Bishop Goodwin could hear the pain and fear in Joc's voice. He continued to let him vent and pace around before he spoke. "What do I do, Bishop, in a situation like this?" Joc asked. "Have a seat, son," Bishop Goodwin said calmly. Joc obeyed and sat down and palmed his face. "You asked how can you right your wrongs. We serve a God of second chances. In most cases third chances, fourth chances, and so on. So firstly, I would advise someone in your situation to repent. You have repented. Now that you have repented, you can turn away from your past and not do those evil things again. Secondly, the streets can't keep you. You are no longer indebted or in bondage to those streets. If the Son sets you free, you will be free indeed. Thirdly, God hasn't given us the spirit of fear. You walk with power now. You were given another chance. God knows you were a no good, messed up, dope pushing, gun happy heathen—" Joc's eyes got big as Bishop Goodwin described the person Joc used to be. "He knew that! And he still chose to give you a second chance. And he knows through you many young men will accept him as their savior because he gave you second chance. So, son, stand up and walk in your power and trust that God is with you every step of the way. If God is for you, who can stand against you? Do you really think he brought you this far to leave you?" Joc sat up straight not really knowing what to say. His spirit man was in total agreeance with his pastor, but his physical man was thinking about the heat from bullets and a crying mother. Bishop Goodwin could still see the worry on Joc's face. "Let me pray for you, son." Bishop Goodwin walked over to Joc and rested his hand on Joc's head. "Dear Heavenly Father, I come to you right now as a covering for your son. I bind and rebuke the spirit of fear. His past can no longer hold him captive. You call him free so the retaliatory spirits must flee. I claim a shield of protection over his life. Because he is your child, no weapon formed against him shall prosper, as he has dropped his bulletproof vest and put on the armor of God. Give him a sound mind as he walks in love and power as you use him as a vessel for those who were once like him. Show him that he can cast his cares on You, Lord, and You will sustain him and he won't be shaken. I know he will do great things that will open doors that no man or devil can shut! Let his spirit be in agreement with mine as he leaves here today with his head held high and a new confidence in You. Oh, Lord, I thank You! And it is so. Amen." Bishop Goodwin patted Joc's shoulder. "It's going to be alright, son." Joc stood up and wiped a tear that rolled down his cheek. "Thank you, Bishop." Joc shook his pastor's hand and walked to the door to leave. "Joc," Bishop Goodwin called him before he walked out. "If you ever need me, I am here." "Thank you, sir." Joc said and exited the office.

Chapter 5

Kincaid paced back and forth yelling and cursing. "Calm down, man!" Joc yelled to match Kincaid's tone. "Calm down? Calm down? Bruh, are you serious?" Kincaid yelled, and then kicked over a trash can. Joc looked around at their burglarized business. All their production equipment was stolen and $200,000 in cash was stolen out of their safe. "When I find out who did this, they good as dead!" Kincaid said, punching the wall. Joc shook his head as his friend continued to go on a rampage. A couple months ago, Joc would have reacted the same way as Kincaid. However, now he doesn't feel that way. To him, it's his confirmation to finally break away from the studio. He actually felt like a burden was lifted off him. Kincaid became calm and stared at his friend. "Why aren't you mad? This is our livelihood and you standing there unbothered!" Kincaid questioned his friend. "Bruh, this hasn't been my livelihood for a while now. And truth be told, this occurrence is the push that I needed to finally walk away," Joc informed Kincaid. "What do you mean?" Kincaid asked confused. "Exactly what it sounds like." Joc said. "Naw, it can't be what it sounds like, because the J.D. I know wouldn't walk away from a business we worked so hard to build," Kincaid said, getting upset all over again. "See, that's the thing. I am no longer J.D. He died. When I was immersed in that water, he was laid to rest. The new me wants no part of this anymore." "Man, you done changed! Them church folks got you out here acting like a weak lil' bit—" Before Kincaid could finish his statement, Joc rushed up to Kincaid grabbing him by his shirt lifting him up and pushing him into the wall. "I may be saved but I am a baby in Christ. Meaning I will still break your face in! Don't ever fix your mouth to disrespect me." Joc let go of Kincaid and stepped back. "You're right, I have changed. You think I've become weak? If anything my new found love for Christ and myself have made me strong. This is not me anymore, from here on out, my money will be made honestly. And although this place is making us money legally, the seed money that planted this building wasn't legal. A bad tree can't produce good fruit, so for that reason, I am out," Joc said, and then took a seat in a nearby chair. Kincaid stared at Joc puzzled. Over the weeks he noticed Joc becoming more distant the more he got involved at his new church home. He thought that maybe Joc going to church would be a short phase and that he would return to being the same old J.D. that he grew up with. But listening to Joc just now he's realizing otherwise. "So you're just going to relinquish your part of the business to me?" Kincaid asked. "Yep, it's all yours, man," Joc said without thought. "But honestly, I think you should walk away from it, too. Not just the studio, but all of it, man. These streets don't love nobody. We know first hand where these streets will take us. Enclosed in a cell or enclosed in a casket." "I know, but I am in so deep, there is no way out for me." Kincaid shook his head. "There is a way out. God is your way out." Joc informed Kincaid. Kincaid rolled his eyes at his friend's comment. "Ain't no way! All the hell I done caused. You know the messed up shit I've done. You really think God will help me? I think not," Kincaid said, dismissing Joc's comment. Joc chuckled at his friend's unbelief. "I was right there with you causing hell but if He did it for me He can do it for you. Come on, man, you are my brother. I can't lose you, to these streets, man. Please, walk away. We can build a new business the honest way and not worry about looking over our shoulders. We above all this, man; God wants us to have better and be better," Joc pleaded suppressing tears. "Nicca, are you about to cry?" Kincaid asked. Joc shook his head and started laughing. Kincaid joined in with laughter. "Sooo, was that what people call a come to Jesus moment?" Kincaid asked in a humorous tone. "Bruh, you are a fool! And yes that was a come to Jesus moment," Joc said, matching his friend's humorous tone but being serious at the same time. The two became silent. Joc, could tell that something was bothering Kincaid. "What's on your mind, man? Joc asked breaking the silence. Kincaid shook his head as to say nothing. He then began to pace the room, and then made a sudden stop and turned to face Joc. He took a deep breath and shook his head again. "Man, look…" Kincaid began but paused. "What is it, man?" Joc asked getting a little annoyed. "We in a little trouble. I didn't want to bother you with this while you were recovering from the shooting. We owe $250000 so I decided to pay off the debt without you even knowing about it. I knew with our new connect and these runners out here moving that paying if off would be nothing. I got word that the new connect were busted, so we weren't able to re-up. Everything we have has been sold and everybody has been paid their share. That also left us enough to pay off the debt. The money that was in the safe was a huge portion for the debt," Kincaid explained. Joc was trying to process the information but none of it made sense to him. "Hold on…What? Who do we owe $250000 to? What did we need $250000 for?" Joc questioned. Kincaid lit a cigarette and took a pull from it, and then exhaled. "Baldo," Kincaid answered. Joc's eyes got big at Kincaid's answer. Many thoughts ran through his mind as to why Kincaid was even dealing with Baldo. After all Baldo is an enemy to them. "Baldo! Are you serious, dude? Baldo? The same Baldo who we just had a nigga knocked off for dealing with-Baldo? Why though? This doesn't make any sense to me," Joc said, waiting on answers from Kincaid. "It's my Mom's debt. She back using that shit again. She knew me, you, or the runners would not sell her anything so she been going to Baldo's people. Anyway, somebody sold her some bad shit, so her crazy ass called the police on the dude who served her. Dude was busted with 6 kilos of cocaine. You know crack-heads run they mouth. Word got back to Baldo that my mom was the one who blew the whistle. Instead of killing her, he came to me for the money. If we don't pay it tomorrow, he coming for us. We gotta come up with this money, our lives are at stake and our moms', man," Kincaid said, pacing the room. Joc never seen Kincaid look so worried. Seldom anything ever fazed Kincaid but clearly, this was bothering him. That alone made Joc become worried. Especially the thought of someone coming after his innocent mother. Joc closed his eyes thinking of what his next move would be. Will he act according to the way his old self would or will he pray and trust God to see him through this? Joc took a long deep breath and opened his eyes. "I got about 50,000 in cash we can put towards it. The other day I seen my pastor with—" Joc said before pausing. He thought about the large amount of money he seen Bishop Goodwin with. "I think I can get us the money. Meet me at my church tomorrow around this time," Joc finished. "Meet you at the church? Are you sure?" Kincaid asked perplexed. "Do you want this money or not?" Joc asked. Kincaid nodded his head. "Yes! I'll be there."

***

It is Wednesday night and Bible class was going on in the sanctuary. Joc excused himself as if he was going to the restroom. Joc looked around and over his shoulder as he stood in front of Bishop Goodwin's office. After seeing that the coast was clear, he turned the doorknob and entered inside. He immediately went to the file cabinet that he had seen Bishop Goodwin put the large amount of money in. Joc picked the lock and found several bank bags filled with money. He stuffed each bag in his pants. As he did this, he heard footsteps in the hallway. He stood still and held his breath. The footsteps continued down the hall. Joc hurried to the office door to leave. As he was about to leave out, he began to feel convicted. He exhaled heavily. "Man, I can't do this," he said to himself. He immediately put the money back in the file cabinet. "Lord, I must really be changing. Me and my Mom's life is on the line. And the money I need is right here. But, I am going to trust You! Lord, I trust You," Joc said, putting his faith to test. Joc slowly walked out of the office and back into the sanctuary. Kincaid texted Joc asking if he got the money. Joc responded by telling him no. Shortly after, Kincaid called Joc's phone repeatedly. Joc ignored the calls trying to figure out a Plan B. Service was over and a few members of the church stayed behind to socialize. Joc went outside to see Kincaid in the parking lot. Kincaid had an uneasy look on his face. "I am sorry, man, I couldn't do it," Joc said, walking up to him. Kincaid swallowed hard and didn't say anything. "Why aren't you saying anything?" Joc asked. "Because we told him to keep his mouth shut!" Baldo said, pointing a gun at the back of Joc's head. Joc stood still. As some of Baldo's goons surrounded Kincaid. "Where is the money?" Baldo asked. "I only have $50000," Joc informed. "Well, I need two-fifty! And I know this church has it, so let's go get it, or I am killing you, him, y'alls mommas, and everybody in that church!" Baldo threatened. "Okay, I'll get the money. Just let me go inside and get it," Joc said, trying to be cooperative. "No, we are all going in," Baldo informed. "Baldo, don't do this, man. Them good people in there. They don't have nothing to do with this," Joc pleaded. "Let's go in!" Baldo demanded pushing Joc towards the church doors with the gun still pointed towards head. The goons grabbed Kincaid and followed Joc and Baldo inside the church. Baldo shoved Joc through the sanctuary doors. Everyone inside jumped and few women screamed. "Don't nobody move!" Baldo said, pointing the gun towards everyone "Or I will kill him." Bishop Goodwin and Deacon Roberts slowly walked up to the men. "Don't come too close!" Baldo warned. "Just take us to the money." Baldo fired a shot in the air and pressed the gun to Joc's temple. "Don't shoot! Please, don't shoot!" Anita screamed through tears. "Shut up, lady!" one of the gunmen yelled. "Take me instead. I'll do whatever you want, but please don't take my baby," she bargained. Bishop Goodwin continued to slowly walk up to Baldo with his hands up. "Don't come any closer, preacher man!" Baldo said, pointing the gun at Bishop Goodwin, and then pushing the metal back to Joc's head. "You don't have to this. There is children and women in here, they don't need to see this. You can have the money, just let him go," Bishop Goodwin reasoned. "Take us to it then!" Baldo demanded. Baldo instructed everyone in the sanctuary to lay on the floor. He left two goons to watch over them. Baldo followed Bishop Goodwin to his office still pointing the gun at Joc. Sister Anita was carried along with them by a third goon. "Hurry up!" Baldo said as Bishop Goodwin got the money out of the file cabinet. "And put the money in a bag." Bishop Goodwin did as he was told. And handed the bag to Baldo. "It's all there. Please let him go." While Baldo was counting the money to see if it was all there, he lost his train of thought. Anita praying out loud kept messing him up. This frustrated Baldo. "Shut up!" Anita continued to pray. Bishop Goodwin began to pray as well as Joc. Baldo heard the sounds of others praying and wailing in the sanctuary. The prayers got louder and louder. The goon that was holding Anita let her go and his face was full of fear. Meanwhile, in the sanctuary the saints were no longer on the floor in fear. Their prayer changed the atmosphere. Deacon Roberts began clapping and giving God praise. The rest of the saints joined in with him. The goons who were ordered to watch them pushed Kincaid to the floor. The clapping and stomping by the saints sounded like thunder, it almost felt as if the room was shaking. "What are they doing?" one goon asked the other. "They're calling in reinforcement… God," the second goon said, losing the color in his face. The first goon aimed his gun at Deacon Roberts. "Be quiet! Make them be quiet. Or I will kill all of you." "If killing a church full of praying people will make you feel better, then do it. Your weapons are formed but they will not prosper. We trust God! And if we die tonight, we will die giving him the glory! Now, do what you gotta do or get out of our church!" Deacon Roberts said loud and boldly. The goon still pointing the gun at Deacon Roberts pulled the trigger. Misfire. The goon fired the gun again…still nothing. "I think it's jammed. Shoot him," he instructed the other goon. The other goon shook his head no and stepped back. "Well, if you don't want to do it, I will!" The goon snatched his partner's gun and tried to fire it. Still, nothing. The goon checked both guns. They were fully loaded with no jams. "What the—" the goon said, confused, looking at Deacon Roberts. "No weapon formed- You know the rest," Deacon Roberts said before rushing towards the goon and wrestling him for the guns. Kincaid and other brothers from the church joined in succeeding in getting the weapons. Four brothers held both goons arms behind their backs. Deacon Roberts and Kincaid were now aiming at the goons to not move. "I guess you go try to shoot us, when clearly they don't work." The goon laughed. Deacon Roberts shook his head. "Excuse me, one moment." Deacon Roberts left the sanctuary to step outside of the church. Once he got outside he fired two shots in the air. He immediately ran back inside. "Did you hear that? It works just fine."

Baldo hearing all the noise from the sanctuary instructed Bishop Goodwin, Joc, and Anita to walk in a line into the sanctuary as him and his goon followed them with their weapons still drawn. Baldo seeing the guns drawn at his goons in the sanctuary instantly grabbed Joc and pulled the trigger. Sister Anita seeing this ran towards Baldo "In the name of Jesus, Satan you must flee!" Bullets fired from all directions. The sanctuary was filled with screams and gunfire, and then silence fell on the room. First Lady Valerie rushed over and kneeled beside Bishop Goodwin who was lying face down on the altar floor. "Oh God, Eugene. Eugene! Baby, say something," she said, rubbing his back. Deacon Roberts who was laying beside Bishop Goodwin slowly got up. "Bishop, are you okay?" Bishop Goodwin lifted his head. "Yes, I don't think I was hit." Bishop Goodwin turned around on his back. First Lady Goodwin looked him down from head to toe. "Oh, thank God!" she said, relieved that he wasn't shot. Deacon Roberts helped him to his feet and Lady Valerie immediately embraced him. Bishop Goodwin held his wife and glanced around the sanctuary. He saw Sister Anita laying over Joc crying. Sister Anita had blood all over her. "Lord, please don't take him now. Please, don't. Please," she sobbed and begged. Bishop Goodwin and First Lady went over to Anita to comfort her and to check on Joc. Anita wouldn't let go of her son for anyone to help. "Mom," Joc mumbled. "Yes, baby I am here." Sister Anita rose up off of Joc. "Mom, was you shot?" Joc noticed the blood on his mother. "No, baby," she answered. "Whose blood is on you?" he asked. She looked at herself, and then Joc who was not bleeding. "O my goodness. This is not your blood. Baby you wasn't shot. Oh, God, thank you!" she said through tears. Bishop Goodwin and Deacon Roberts helped Anita and Joc stand up. After scanning around the church making sure all the saints were unharmed, they discovered Baldo was killed by Kincaid. All the goons were shot as well but not killed. Several ambulance and police arrived to the church. Police took everyone's statement as the paramedics helped the injured. Kincaid was hit in the shoulder but was expected to be alright. As Kincaid was being wheeled out on a stretcher, Joc ran up to him. "Bruh! You go be alright, man. You hear me?" Joc assured him. "Yeah, I know. I am a fighter," Kincaid said, forcing a smile through his pain. "Thank you, man! You took that bullet for me. You stood up for me like a true brother." "Naw, man, you stood by me like a true brother. I got us in this mess. You could have turned your back on me and left me to figure it out. But you didn't, so I should be thanking you. Thank you for opening my eyes up to see who God really is. If I never came here tonight I wouldn't have witnessed the true work of God. Man! I will never forget this night. Joc, man, I am ready to do right. This will not be the last time I step foot inside this church. Next time I am here, I will be here for the right reasons..." Joc smiled ear to ear at his friend's words. Joc raised his hands and lifted his head back, filled with praise. "Psalms 28:7 says: 'The LORD *is* my strength and my shield; my heart trusted in him, and I am helped: therefore my heart greatly rejoiceth; and with my song will I praise him.' In spite of what it looks like, in spite of what it feels like, I will trust you for the rest of my life. Thank you for keeping me."

A Broken Vow

Chapter 1

"Good morning, my love!" Shalon greeted her husband, Rodney, as he came in the kitchen. "Good morning, babe," he replied as he gave her a hug and kiss on the forehead. "What's for breakfast? I am starving!" Rodney told his wife. "Smoothies!" Shalon said as she placed spinach, strawberries, bananas, and orange juice in a blender. Rodney grimaced at the look of the green mixture as it was being blended. Shalon laughed at the face her husband made. "You will like it, trust me!" she assured him. "I trust you, babe. But uhhh...I was hoping for some bacon and eggs," Rodney said as Shalon handed him a glass of the green smoothie. "Just drink it, silly! I will make you an awesome dinner tonight!" Shalon said playfully. "Ooh wee, I can't wait!" Rodney said as he pulled Shalon close holding her by the waist. "Well, babe, I got to get out of here before I am late for work," Rodney told his wife. "And I may be running a little late this evening." "Again?" Shalon said, feeling a little disappointed. Lately, Rodney has been coming home late due to the added responsibilities that come with his new position as a marketing manager. "Yes, again. I am sorry, babe. I will make it up to you tomorrow night. We can have a little date night and little night cap if you know what I mean," Rodney said, grinning. Shalon couldn't help but laugh at her husband's gesture. One thing Shalon loves about Rodney is his sense of humor. He keeps her laughing at the littlest things. "I just miss you!" Shalon said in a baby voice giving him a sad face. Shalon suddenly remembered that tomorrow night the praise team is meeting up for rehearsal at church. Shalon has always loved to sing. When she was a young, girl her grandmother would have her sing in front of the church and for her friends at the beauty salon. Everyone would tell her that she had such a powerful voice to be a little girl. "Oh, I just remembered tomorrow I have rehearsal at church," Shalon told Rodney. "Well, babe, we will work something out," he assured her. He gave her a hug and kiss before heading towards the door to leave. "Hey, don't forget your smoothie!" Shalon stopped Rodney before he walked out the door. "Thanks, babe! I love you," Rodney told his wife and kissed her once again. "Love you, too! Have a good day," Shalon responded. She watched Rodney leave the house and enter his car. He blew his horn and waved at her as he backed out of the driveway. Shalon waved back and closed the front door. She then headed upstairs to her and Rodney's bedroom to get dressed for her morning walk. She put on a gray racer back tee, black yoga pants, and running shoes. After getting dressed, she looked in the mirror and pulled her honey brown colored hair into a high ponytail and applied some lip balm. Shalon has a short, petite shapely stature. She is fair skinned and has hazel eyes. She is a pleasure to be around and always full of joy and laughter. But she is also a firecracker and can go from 0 to 100 real quick.

"Lady!" she called for her Pomeranian pooch. "Come on, Lady, it's time for your morning walk." Lady came running down the hallway to Shalon's command. "Hey, mama's baby!" she said to the pooch as she scooped her in her arms to put her leash on. Shalon then grabbed her earbuds and phone and headed outside. *It feels so good out today,* Shalon thought. The sun was shining and there was a light breeze. She immediately began to power walk. Shalon loves working out. She takes a four-mile walk every morning and goes to the gym 5 days a week. While walking, Shalon likes to listen to Christian and Contemporary gospel music. One, she gets to praise and worship; two, she prays as well; three, it takes her mind off the fact that she is walking four miles; and four, it gets her so pumped up and ready for her day. One of Shalon's favorite songs began to play 'Solid Rock' by Tasha Cobb. Shalon sang along with the track out loud. "Yasss, Jesus!" she clapped her hands. *Jesus, you are so amazing!* she thought to herself. Lady began to bark at another dog, which took Shalon out of her thoughts. "It's okay, baby," Shalon said to the pooch to calm her down. The owner of the other dog waved at Shalon. Shalon waved back and noticed it was one of her neighbors, Mr. Jefferies, who lived a few houses down from her. "Pretty day, huh?" Mr. Jefferies asked. "Yes, it is. I love this weather we have been having lately," Shalon told him. "How is Mrs. Jefferies doing?" Shalon asked. "She is well, she had shoulder surgery a couple days ago, so she can't get out in the garden like she wants to. But she is feeling a lot better." Mr. Jefferies informed her. "Send her my well wishes, and I know she will be back out in her garden in no time," Shalon said. "I will tell her you asked about her. Enjoy the rest of your day," Mr. Jefferies said before he continued his walk with his dog. "You, too, Mr. Jefferies," Shalon said as she put her ear buds back in her ears. She glanced at her phone and noticed the time. *Oh, my I need to hurry up and get back home,* Shalon thought. She has to be at work in an hour and it usually takes her an hour to get ready. So, instead of power walking back home, she jogged. Which wore poor Lady out. As soon as they walked in the door, Lady ran to her doggy bed and lay out. Shalon laughed at her pooch's action. "I guess Momma wore you out this morning." Shalon headed back to her room so she could get ready for work. She took a quick shower, applied her makeup, put her hair in a sleek ponytail, and put on a business casual outfit with some pumps. She grabbed her purse and keys and headed to the kitchen. She filled Lady's food pans with food and water. Then grabbed her lunch out of the fridge that she prepared the night before. She petted Lady on the head and left out the house and entered her car. She has 10 minutes to get to work. But she knew she wouldn't get there on time being that she lives 20 minutes away and that's not including traffic time. She is never late, so when she called her boss to let him know she is running behind, he didn't make a big deal and told her to be safe and take her time. Shalon is an accountant at a small accounting firm. She loves what she does and is going into her fifth year with the company. Shalon finally pulls into her place of employment's parking lot. Her usual parking space was taken so she had to park further from the building. *I guess I picked the wrong day to wear heels,* she thought to herself as she walked to the building. Once inside, she got on the elevator to get to the fifth floor. When she got off the elevator, she went straight to her cubicle instead of stopping at the break room to make coffee like she usually does. She was welcomed with tons of emails and voicemails. Shalon immediately began to respond to her emails, return missed calls, and got started on her objectives for the day. "Good morning, Shalon, I didn't know you made it in already," Shalon's boss Ian Cassidy said, noticing her hard at work in her cubicle. "Good morning, Mr. Cassidy. I guess I snuck in and got right to work," Shalon said. "Do you have a second? I would like to talk to you for a moment," Mr. Cassidy asked. "Yes, sure," Shalon answered. "Great. Come with me to my office." He motioned her to follow him. Shalon's mind began to wander all over the place. *Am I getting called into his office because I am late? Because I am never late. That surely can't be the reason. Did I meet all my deadlines last week? Did I fumble some numbers? What can it be?* "Have a seat, Shalon," Mr. Cassidy insisted. Shalon sat down in anticipation of why she was called in there. "So you are probably wondering why I pulled you away from your many tasks. Well, I thought you needed a break. Because everyone around here knows if it was up to you, you wouldn't take your breaks or lunch," he said with a humorous tone. "I guess I can be a busy worker bee at times," Shalon said as she watched Mr. Cassidy pull out a big manila envelope and pull out some paperwork. "Exactly, and that's why I called you in here. You are such a hard worker. You have gotten excellent performance reviews since you've been with the company and you exceed and go the extra mile in all you do. I can always count on you and for that reason, I want to promote you to Senior Accountant," Mr. Cassidy informed Shalon. "Omigod! Are you serious?" Shalon said, very surprised. "Yes! Here is your offer letter, please take a look at it. If you choose to accept the offer, it will go into effect immediately," Mr. Cassidy said as he handed her the offer letter. "Thank you so much! I am almost speechless," Shalon said, staring at the offer letter. "No, thank you for all you do! You deserve this," Mr. Cassidy assured Shalon. Shalon took the letter and went back to her cubicle. Shalon read over the offer and was pleased to see that her job description was almost exactly the same as her current position except with a $10000 pay increase and a separate office. Without a second thought, Shalon raised her hands and said, "Hallelujah! Thank you Jesus!"

Chapter 2

On her way home from work, Shalon stopped at the grocery store to grab a few items for dinner. She remembered Rodney wasn't too pleased with the idea of having a smoothie for breakfast earlier. So, staying true to her word, she is going to prepare him an awesome dinner. His favorite: steak, shrimp, a fully loaded baked potato, roasted vegetables and dinner rolls. Also, before she went home, she stopped and picked up a bottle of red wine to celebrate her promotion. Finally home, Shalon kicked off her pumps and placed the groceries on the counter. She was immediately greeted by Lady. "Hey, Lady baby! I missed you, Momma's baby," Shalon said, hugging the pooch. Shalon let Lady go run out in the yard to do her business and let out some energy. Shalon then went upstairs to change into some comfortable clothes, and then rushed downstairs to prepare dinner. Shalon put on some music and poured her a glass of wine. As she made dinner, she danced around the kitchen and sung along to Corinne Bailey Rae's 'Put Your Records On.' Dinner is almost ready, so Shalon began to set the table. She looked up at the kitchen clock to see how much time she has left before Rodney comes home. It is 6:30. Usually, Rodney is home around 5:30 or 6:00. *Hopefully, he is home around seven,* Shalon thought knowing he would be a little late this evening. She finished setting the table and decided to call Rodney. "You have reached, Rodney Harris, sorry I missed you, please leave a brief message and I will get back to you shortly," Rodney's voicemail greeting played. Shalon disconnected the call and dialed him once more. The call went straight to voicemail again. "Really?" Shalon said frustrated. She finished her glass of wine and tried calling his office phone. Still no answer. *Maybe his cell is dead,* Shalon thought. To keep herself busy, she decided to tidy up the house a bit. Shalon heard tapping at her front door. It was Lady, Shalon forgot that she had let her out. "Oh, Lady bug! I am so sorry," she said as she let Lady back inside the house. As she let Lady in, Rodney pulled up into the driveway. *About time,* Shalon thought noticing it was now 7:30. "Hey, babe!" Rodney said as he walked up to the door. Shalon greeted him with a hug and kiss. "How was your day?" she asked. "Busy, but productive. How was yours?" he responded. "It was great!" she told him. "Good! I am glad you had a great day. Mmm... What you got cooking in here? It smells amazing." Rodney said as he walked into the kitchen. "Your fave." Shalon smiled taking his hand and leading him into the dining room.

"I told you I was going to make you an awesome dinner tonight." "Ooh, I am ready! Babe, I am starving; that smoothie left me as soon as I swallowed it and I skipped lunch today. So give me double portions of everything," Rodney said, taking off his sports coat as he took a seat at the dining room table. "Good thing I made plenty. Here you are, sir," Shalon said as she placed Rodney's plate in front of him. "Yes, God!" he said at the sight of dinner. Shalon then poured them both a glass of wine and set across from her husband. "Lord, thank You for this meal we are about to receive, let it be a nourishment to our bodies, and bless my beautiful wife for preparing it," Rodney blessed the food. "Amen," they said in unison. "Wine tonight? What's the occasion?" he asked. Shalon smiled and shared the good news she received earlier. "I got a promotion today! You are now looking at the new Senior Accountant at Cassidy and Bailey's CPA Firm." "That's awesome, babe! Come here," he said as he reached out to give her a hug. "This is excellent news! You deserve it, baby," he told her as he held her and spun her around. "Thank you! The best part is, my job description is basically the same but it includes a nice pay raise and I get my own office," she shared. "Uh-oh! You moving on up, no more cubicle action for you, girl," Rodney joked. "But real talk, babe,

I am happy for you," Rodney said on a more serious note. "It's amazing how the Lord has shown us both favor in our careers. I mean we both got promotions within weeks of each other," Shalon said of their new blessings. "You are right and I am so thankful," Rodney agreed. As they ate their dinner, Rodney's phone rang. He took his phone out of his pocket and silenced it. "Who was that?" Shalon asked. "Work. Brad is still there working on marketing strategies for a new restaurant that's about to have a grand opening soon. I will call him back after dinner," Rodney answered. His phone rang again. "Work again?" Shalon asked. Rodney looked at his phone and nodded his head yes. "Go ahead a take it, babe," Shalon said as she got up to take their plates to the kitchen sink. "This is Rodney," Rodney answered his phone and walked to the living room to take the call. Shalon finished clearing the dining room table and loaded the dishwasher. Rodney came into the kitchen to help her clean up. "Was everything alright at work?" she asked "Yes. Brad isn't the sharpest tool in the shed. I just had to walk him through a few things." Rodney explained. "Hey, let's watch a movie together. Tomorrow is going to be a long day for me and I know you got rehearsal at the church tomorrow night. I want to spend as much time with you as possible before our schedules get out of sync," Rodney suggested. "Sure, I would love that. What are you in the mood to watch?" Shalon said as they went to the living room. "No chick flicks or anything on Lifetime," he said, pulling up the t.v. guide on the television. "I agree! I don't want to see you get all emotional and in your feelings," Shalon joked as she threw a decorative pillow at him. "Aw, OK, you got jokes tonight, I see. Just for that, I am about to put on the most action-packed macho film I can find," Rodney said as he threw the pillow back at Shalon. Shalon shook her head no and frowned at the thought of watching an action movie. Rodney laughed at his wife's disinterest. "Well, you know we can always make our own movie." Rodney smiled and winked. *Oh my goodness. What am I going to do with this man?* Shalon thought as she stared at her handsome husband. Rodney looks as if he walked straight out of a GQ magazine. He is tall and has an athletic build and keeps a sharp goatee and fade. Shalon loves everything about his appearance but she is a sucker for his soulful eyes and smile. "Our own movie, huh?" she played along. "Yeah! You down?" he said, rubbing his chin. "But I am not that type of girl," she said, biting her finger playing the shy-innocent role. "It's all good, I won't tell anybody," he said, pulling her near him. "You promise?" she said as he begins to kiss her neck. Shalon instantly fell out of the playful-shy character she was portraying. She closed her eyes as her whole body warmed up. Rodney gently bit her lip, and then kissed her intensely. Shalon pushed him back to the sofa and got on top of him to straddle him. She unbuttoned his shirt, and then took off hers. As things begin to escalate, Rodney picked Shalon up and carried her to their bedroom and turned off the lights.

***

Shalon woke up to Lady whimpering outside her bedroom door. Shalon looked at her alarm clock. It is 3:30 a.m. *She's probably whimpering because she needs to go outside,* Shalon thought. Shalon got out of bed and put on her robe and slippers. As soon as she opened her bedroom door, Lady started nipping at her feet, and then started running in circles, and subsequently proceeded to the front door to be let out. When Shalon let Lady out, she noticed that Rodney's car wasn't in the driveway. Her first thought was that someone stole his car. She immediately went back to their bedroom and noticed he was not in the bed, she then looked in their bedroom bathroom and he wasn't there either. *Surely he didn't leave without telling me,* she thought. She continued to search for him around the house to no avail. She went into the kitchen where he left his keys and wallet earlier and saw that they were no longer there. "Where can he be at this hour?" she said to herself. She picked up their home phone and gave him a call. She called him three times with no answer. She grabbed her cell phone and texted him. "Babe, where are you?" she texted. She waited a couple of minutes for a reply. No reply. "I am worried. Please respond or call me back ASAP," she sent another text message. "I am okay, babe! I just decided to go to the gym," he finally texted back. "The gym! At this hour?" she responded back. "Yes, babe. With me having to work late so much now this is the only time I can get my workouts in. I am about to leave now," he sent a final text. Her woman's intuition called bull crap at his whereabouts, but she dismissed it due to the fact that he is a gym rat. And now that he works longer hours, it has been interfering with his gym schedule. Shalon decided to not overthink things. She let Lady back inside and went back to her bedroom. Shalon got back in the bed but lay there wide-awake. She reached for her phone and logged into her Facebook account and, out of boredom, begins to like random posts and photos. As she scrolled through her timeline, she saw a photo that her husband is tagged in. Shalon didn't recognize the person who tagged him in it. So she clicked on the tagger's name to view his profile. It turns out the guy who tagged Rodney is a photographer. From viewing the photographer's profile, it seems like he only takes pictures of people at bars and clubs, and then post and tags them in it. The photo Rodney is tagged in was posted an hour ago. Shalon studied the photo but couldn't tell where Rodney was. He was alone in the photo sitting at a table with a few shot glasses. Mad that Rodney lied about being at the gym, she went downstairs to the living room to wait on him to come home. She didn't have to wait too long because as soon as she entered the living room, she heard Rodney's keys rattling as he unlocked the door. Rodney opened the door to Shalon standing there with her arms crossed looking very angry. "Where have you been? You were not at the gym!" she questioned him loudly. "What are you talking about? I told you I was at the gym," he said confused. "What is this then?" she shoved her phone in his face so that he can see the picture of him. "Babe, that photo was taken last week at a new club that I helped out with marketing. Me and a few other colleagues went there for the grand opening." Rodney informed her. Shalon tried to remember if he mentioned marketing for a new club last week but she couldn't recall. She began to calm down as she noticed he had on his gym clothes. "Babe, I was at the gym. I wouldn't lie to you," he assured her. Shalon begin to feel bad for assuming he lied about his whereabouts without all the facts. "I am sorry, Rodney. I...I just woke up to you not being here. It seemed very odd for you to be at the gym at this time. And to see that photo of you posted on Facebook around the same time had me seeing red," Shalon said, feeling remorseful. "I can see how this could be mistaken for what it's not. But it's all good," he told her. "I would give you a hug but I am little sweaty and funky," he said, and then kissed her on the forehead. "I love you. I am about to get showered," Rodney told her. "I love you, too," Shalon said as Rodney made his way upstairs.

A few hours have passed, Rodney is in his home office working on his laptop before he leaves for work. Shalon put Lady's leash on so they can take their routine morning walk. Once outside, Shalon saw that Rodney left his car windows down. When she watched their local news earlier, rain was forecasted for today. Shalon got into Rodney's car to let up his windows. As she was letting the windows up, she looked at his backseat and found a duffle bag with clothes hanging out of it. Shalon grabbed the bag and pulled out the articles of clothing: a buttoned-down shirt, some slacks, a tie, and some dress shoes. The same outfit that was worn in the picture he was tagged in. She also found a few receipts. She put the clothes back in the duffle bag and placed the bag back on the backseat. She kept the receipts and shoved them in her jacket pocket. Not wanting to go back in and confront Rodney about it, she continued as normal with her morning walk.

Chapter 3

Shalon went about her morning as usual. After her morning walk, she made breakfast and lunch for her and Rodney, she filled up Lady's food and water pans and then got ready for work. As soon as Shalon got to work, she met with Mr. Cassidy to accept the promotion that was offered to her. Most of her work day was spent with HR changing her title and filling out paperwork. Next, she had to wait on the IT department to come to her new office to set up her phone and computer. Shalon then had to move all her belongings from her old cubicle to her new office. Shalon is finally set up in her new office. It's not that big, but it beats the cubicles plus it has a window. She set at her desk and managed to get some work done. After resolving some discrepancies on an account she was analyzing, her mind began to drift to Rodney. She wants to believe his story of being at the gym so bad. But the photo on Facebook and the clothes in his car say otherwise. Shalon reached for her purse and took out the receipts she found in Rodney's duffle bag. One of the receipts was from an establishment named Bar Red, where a one hundred dollar tab in drinks was run up. The second receipt was from an establishment called Euphoria where another one hundred dollars was spent on drinks. Both receipts are dated from last night. *Where are these places and why did he spend so much money on drinks?* Shalon thought. She didn't want to search for these places on her work computer, so she did a search on her phone. She opened up her web browser and typed into the search engine Bar Red. The search returned an address and phone number and had it classified as a bar. Shalon took a deep breath as she typed in Euphoria into the search engine. Everything in her told her that this may be a gentlemen's club. *Here goes nothing* she thought as she hit search. Shalon put her head down with her hand over her face and clinched her other hand into a fist. After sitting there for a few moments taking deep breaths to keep calm, she picked up her phone to finish looking at the web search results for Euphoria. It was, in fact, a gentlemen's club. She screened shot the address for future reference. Her eyes began to well up with tears and she felt a huge lump in her throat as she tried to suppress them. Shalon couldn't tell which hurt most, the fact that Rodney lied to her or the fact that he spent his night in a strip club. Shalon regained her composure and decided to go ahead and end her work day. She gathered her things and headed for the elevator.

Shalon felt as if the elevator was taking forever to get to the first floor. She was beginning to feel closed in and became lightheaded. Once the elevator door opened on the first floor, she walked out as fast as she could. She didn't slow down until she got to her car. She started up her car, backed out of her parking space, and then sped out of the parking lot. She eventually had to slow down once she got onto the road due to rush hour traffic, which made Shalon even more frustrated. Her phone began to vibrate. She looked down at it since she was currently at a standstill in traffic. It was Spencer, he is the praise and worship leader at her church and also her best friend. He was texting her a reminder about rehearsal that night. She responded back that she was on her way to the church.

About thirty minutes later, Shalon pulled up to the church. She didn't get out right away; instead, she tried to clear her mind. One thing she didn't want to do was go into the church feeling or looking unhappy. Especially since this is one of her happy places. "Jesus, help me," she said as she got out of her car. She entered the church and made her way into the sanctuary. The musicians were already rehearsing some new music. The other praise members were looking at the lyrics to some songs that

Spencer passed out. "Well, look who is here. Please come join us," Spencer said when he noticed Shalon. "Long day?" Spencer asked as he handed Shalon a sheet with lyrics. "I guess you can say that, but that didn't stop me from coming here to make a joyful noise with you guys," she said, trying not to seem like anything is bothering her. "Amen to that!" Spencer said as everyone else joined in. "Okay, now that we are all here, let's get started with prayer," Spencer said as he led the group in prayer. After looking over the lyrics, listening to the original songs, and reciting it several times, the praise team went up to the pulpit to sing. They were practicing the song 'We are Victorious' by Donnie McClurkin featuring Tye Tribbett. It is an upbeat song, so the team was able to rock, jump, clap, and dance. The next song they rehearsed was 'Joy' by Vashawn Mitchell which isn't as upbeat as the other song but perfect for worship. When rehearsal came to an end, Spencer once again led the group in prayer before they went their separate ways. "Great job, guys! I will see you all later this week," Spencer said as a few of the members left. "Is everything okay?" Spencer asked Shalon as they walked to the back of the sanctuary. "Yes. Why do you ask?" Shalon replied. "I've known you too long, you don't seem like yourself today," he said concerned. "Really? I am fine. As a matter of fact, I got a nice promotion today!" she told him. "That's great! Congrats!" he said, giving her a high five. "Well, I know you are probably in a rush to get home to Rodney. So let me walk you to your car," Spencer said, opening the sanctuary door for Shalon. He noticed Shalon didn't say anything to his comment and asked her once again if she was okay. She assured him she was fine and just tired. They said their goodbyes once Shalon got into her car. It is 8:30 and Shalon wondered if Rodney was home yet. She was about to call him but stopped herself. Instead, she decided to drive home in silence. When she got home, she saw Rodney's car in the driveway. She pulled up next to his car and got out to go inside the house. When she entered their home, she could smell that Rodney cooked dinner. She also found a dozen roses in a beautiful vase sitting on the living room coffee table. She read the card next to the roses. 'Congratulations Mrs. Senior Accountant! I love you, Rodney.' "Hey, Babe!" Rodney came into the living room. Shalon turned around to acknowledge him. "Hi! Thank you, these are beautiful," she said, referring to the roses. "I am glad you like them. I hope you are hungry. You made my favorite last night so I made your favorite tonight. Chicken marsala and pasta," he said, walking up to her and placing a kiss on her forehead. "It smells wonderful," she managed to smile. "Well, come on girl let's eat," he said, taking her by the hand and leading her into the dining room. He pulled out her chair so that she can be seated. He placed both of their plates on the table and poured them both a glass of white wine. He sat down and asked about her day. Shalon carried on as if nothing was bothering her. She told him all about her work day and the new songs she learned at rehearsal. She even managed to laugh at all his jokes even though she didn't find him to be humorous at the moment. After dinner, Shalon and Rodney decided to call it a night. They tidied up the kitchen, prepared for their work day for the following day, and went to bed.

A few hours have passed. Shalon was awakened by the sound of a car ignition starting up. She turned over in bed to find that Rodney wasn't there. The bathroom light in their bedroom was not on, so she knew he wasn't in there. Shalon thought about the car ignition she just heard. She jumped out of bed to see if Rodney's car is still in the driveway. She looked out her bedroom window and to her dismay, Rodney's car was not there. "Let me guess, he's at the gym?" she said to herself sarcastically. Wanting to get to the bottom of what's really going on with Rodney, Shalon decided to go out and find him. She put on the first thing she could find—a pink and black tracksuit and Ugg boots. She grabbed her phone, keys, and purse and headed to her car. Once she got into her car, she put the address to Euphoria in her GPS system. The whole drive she prayed that Rodney wasn't there. She was navigated to the location, which was in the downtown area of their city. The establishment had a nice size parking lot, so she drove around it a few times to see if she could find Rodney's vehicle. Sure enough, she spotted his vehicle. Just to be sure she drove close enough to read the license plate. Rodney has a custom made license plate that says HOT ROD. And this indeed was his car that she is looking at. She found a parking space where she can see him when he comes out without her being seen. About one hour has passed, and then Shalon saw a woman exit the building. She had on gold high waisted leggings, a black bustier, and black knee-high stiletto boots. The woman was carrying a large bag. Shalon automatically assumed the woman was a stripper and that she was ending her night. Soon after, a man joined the woman. He stood behind her and wrapped his arms around her waist. The woman moved her hair to one side of her shoulder so that the man could kiss her neck. Shalon squinted her eyes to get a good look at the man. It was Rodney! He was all over the woman groping and fondling her. The woman seemed to be enjoying it because she was smiling and fondling him as well. Shalon was watching her worse nightmare play out. After knowing Rodney for ten years and being married to him for six, she never thought he would betray her like this. Shalon's heart felt as if it dropped to her stomach and all of a sudden, she had shortness of breath. "No! No! Lord Why?" she shouted. Tears filled her eyes. Everything in her wanted to get out of her car and slap the crap out of Rodney and demand answers. But she stayed inside and watched Rodney and the woman get into his vehicle. Rodney drove away from the location. Shalon waited a moment, and then followed behind him. She didn't want him to notice her so she allowed a couple of cars to pass in front of her. The drive was short. Rodney turned into a hotel and parked. He opened the passenger door for the woman to help her out. They proceeded into the hotel. Shalon felt she had seen enough and left the hotel. She cried the whole way home. She could barely see through her tears that she passed multiple red lights. She managed to make it home safely. When she got inside the house, she let all her emotions out. She went to the living room, grabbed the vase of roses that Rodney gave her earlier and threw it across the room. The vase hit the wall and shattered into many pieces. She then went into the kitchen and made herself a glass of wine, she drank it fast as if it was a shot, and then she threw the wine glass as hard as she could causing it to break as well. She screamed to the top of her lungs, and then grabbed the rest of the bottle of wine and took it straight to the head, finishing it all. She continued to break dishes and punched the walls. Lady was terrified and began to bark and whimper at Shalon's actions. Out of breath and drained Shalon picked up Lady and sat on the floor and cried until she fell asleep.

Chapter 4

It was a little after five in the morning when Rodney came home. The house was a mess. Everywhere he stepped there was glass. He walked around with caution because deep down inside he knew that Shalon knew what he has been up to. "Babe!" he called out to her. "Babe, where are you?" he began to look around the house for her. He found her sleeping with Lady on the floor in their upstairs hallway. He walked up and kneeled beside her. "Babe." He shook her arm to wake her. Shalon woke up with the worse headache. She looked around and wondered why she was on the floor. She looked at Rodney and the images of him with another woman came back to her remembrance. He helped her up. Once Shalon was standing on her feet, she leaned back and punched Rodney in the face. Before he could stop her, she punched him again and pushed him continuously. "How could you do this to me? What did I do to deserve this? Answer me! Answer me!" she shouted. "Stop, baby! Calm down. Let's talk about this," Rodney said as he grabbed Shalon to restrain her. Shalon may be small but she is very strong. She broke away from his grip and slapped him. Tired of the free licks she was getting, Rodney picked Shalon up, carried her to their room and slammed her on their bed. "I said stop, dammit!" he yelled at her. Pinned down and unable to move, Shalon yelled back at him "Go to hell! You are dead to me!" "Shalon, calm down." "Get off of me Rodney! I hate you! I hate you!" Shalon began to sob. Rodney looked at his wife as she sobbed louder. "Babe, I am going to get off you. But you have to promise to stay calm and talk to me. Deal?" he told her. "Do we have a deal?" he asked. Tired of fighting and unable to move under Rodney's weight, she agreed. Rodney got off of her and helped her up. He sat on the edge of the bed with his head down. Shalon stood in front of him. "Why, Rodney, and how long has this been going on?" she asked. He didn't respond. "You said you want to talk! So talk, I need answers!" she shouted. He looked up at her and finally answered her. "I met her at one of the clubs I was advertising for a few weeks ago; she came on to me. After a few drinks, I felt weak." "So it was that easy for you to throw your whole marriage away?" Shalon questioned him. "Baby, I am sorry," he apologized. "Yeah, you are sorry. Sorry you got caught!" she said, pushing his forehead back with her index finger. Rodney jumped up and grabbed her wrist. "Look, I admit I was wrong. And yes you hate me right now, but this is the last time you are going to put your hands on me." He warned her. "Or what? You're going to hit me? Go ahead, hit me! I mean the damage is done. You already caused me so much pain, you hitting me won't even faze me at this point," Shalon said, jerking away from his grasp. "Just leave! Get out, get your shit and get out!" Shalon yelled. "This is my house, too, and I am not going anywhere!" Rodney said just as loud. The doorbell rang and they both got silent. Lady was downstairs barking at the doorbell ringing. Rodney looked out the bedroom window to see who could be at the door, he couldn't tell. So Shalon went downstairs and opened the front door. It was Mrs. Jefferies who lived a few houses down. "Hi, Shalon. Is everything okay? I was taking a walk and heard a lot of commotion coming out of here," Mrs. Jefferies asked concern. "Who is at the door?" Rodney asked as he came and joined Shalon at the door. "Hello, Mrs. Jefferies," Rodney acknowledged her. "Yes, everything is fine," Shalon assured her. Mrs. Jefferies stared at Shalon, and then glanced at Rodney. Mrs. Jefferies leaned in towards Shalon and whispered, "Are you sure, honey?" Shalon nodded her head yes. Mrs. Jefferies glanced at Rodney again. "Well, okay, you guys have a good day," she said, and then whispered to Shalon again, "Call me if you need me." Mrs. Jefferies left their property and Shalon closed the door. She turned around and Rodney was still standing there. "She probably thinks I was in here beating you," Rodney said, shaking his head. "That's what it feels like. I am in so much pain emotionally that I feel like I've taking a beating physically," Shalon said as tears rolled down her face. She wiped her eyes and headed to the staircase to make her way up to their bedroom. Rodney stopped her before she could. They were facing each other but Shalon was looking past him to avoid eye contact. "I love you," Rodney told her. Shalon pushed past him. "Whatever. I am about to get ready for work. Do not be here when I get back. I am pretty sure there is plenty of vacancies at the hotel you were at last night. But um… it's check out time here," Shalon made her way upstairs. She heard the front door shut as Rodney left the house. She watched out their bedroom window as he entered his car and drove away.

With everything that has transpired, Shalon still managed to make it to work on time. It was definitely a struggle, though. The constant tears, not wanting to move, and when she did move, it was as if she was moving in slow motion. She sat at her desk unmotivated to get started on her task. *I just need to get through this day and then it's the weekend,* she thought. She opened her music app on her phone and put it on gospel radio. She closed her eyes as the song 'Healing' by Kelly price ministered to her. Tears filled her eyes and she began to pray that the Lord gets her through this trying time. After that, she was able to get through her work day. Once her work day ended, she went to a bar and grill type of establishment. She hadn't eaten all day so she decided to grab a quick bite. She went over the menu and realized that it was happy hour. She ordered two margaritas to go along with her meal. She felt a little tipsy after drinking both margaritas and knew if she had another drink that would be pushing it. However, she ended up ordering two cranberry vodka cocktails. She drank both cocktails fast, paid her ticket, and left a tip. She left the establishment and got into her car. *I shouldn't be driving*, she thought. She began to laugh, and then cry. "Four drinks and I am still crying?" she said to herself. She got out of her car and walked to a bar that is beside the bar and grill she just left. She went inside and ordered a couple of tequila shots and a beer. When she was done drinking, she thought about Rodney. No tears came this time but anger did. She hit the table with her fist causing several patrons inside the bar to look at her. "What are you staring at? Carry on!" she yelled at the onlookers. She grabbed her purse and exited the bar. She stumbled as she walked to her car and she felt as if the world was spinning. It is now dark outside. *I need to get home,* she thought. "I can't drive!" she said of her drunkenness. She pulled out her phone and pressed down on the home button for her virtual assistant. "Call Spencer," she spoke into the phone. "Calling Spencer," the virtual assistant responded. Shalon waited for Spencer to answer. After a while of only hearing the phone ring, she hung up. She looked at the time. She realized Spencer did not pick up his phone because it is Friday night prayer at the church. "I am missing prayer," she said with her speech slurred. She started up the ignition to head to the church. She took back roads to avoid being around other motorists. She drove super slow. Her eyes were heavy and her vision was blurry. "Jesus, get me to the church safely," she said of the danger she put herself and others in. She arrived at the church. "Thank you, Jesus!" she said as she parked. She tried calling Spencer again. "Hey, there!" he answered. "Spencer! Hey Spencer," she said, excited that he picked up. "Shalon? Are you okay?" he asked noticing her voice sounds different. "Is prayer still going on?" she asked loudly. "Yes. Why are you so loud?" he asked. "Because I am drunk!" she blurted out and started laughing. "Where are you?" Spencer asked concerned. "I am out here in the parking lot. Come outside," she slurred. Spencer looked around to make sure no one was listening to him on the phone call. He exited the church and went to Shalon's car. Shalon saw Spencer making his way over. So she got out of her car. She was stammering and lost her balance. Spencer ran up and caught her before she fell. "Hey Spencer!" she said in a baby voice as he caught her. "Shalon, what's going on?" he said, holding her up and trying to keep her on her feet. "I've never seen you like this. And I can't believe you drove while under the influence. What were you thinking?" he continued. She put her arms around Spencer's shoulders to stay balanced. She pressed her nose against his nose and laughed. Spencer looked around to make sure none of the saints have come out. "Shalon! We can't let anyone see you like this," he said quietly but in a serious tone. "I am taking you home. Give me your keys," Spencer instructed. Shalon handed over her keys and Spencer led Shalon to his car. He helped her get in the car and then drove her home. Spencer went inside the house with her to try to get an understanding of what is going on with her. Shalon kicked her shoes off and went to the kitchen. Spencer observed the mess the house was in. Roses sitting in a puddle of water on the floor, the broken vase, and crooked pictures on the whole. Shalon came out of the kitchen drinking right from a wine bottle. "Have a seat! Make yourself at home," She said, making her way into the living room. "No! I will not let you do this. You've had enough," Spencer said, taking the bottle away from her. Shalon tripped and fell trying to take the bottle back. Spencer took the bottle and poured the wine down the kitchen sink. "Hey! Why would you do that? I was drinking that," she said, annoyed, trying to get up off the floor. "You don't need it. What happened in here? It's a mess. Did you and Rodney have a fight?" Spencer asked of the state the house was in. Shalon looks up at Spencer with her now red glassy eyes. She was silent but the hurt she was feeling was all over her face. "Spence... Rod- Rodney... He ch—" she choked trying to get the words out. "He cheated," she finally managed to say. Spencer closed his eyes and shook his head. He kneeled before her to give her a hug. "Shalon, I am so sorry. Lord knows you don't deserve this," he comforted her. She hugged Spencer back and buried her face in his chest as she cried. "It's going to be okay. You can use my shoulder as long as you need," he said, rubbing her back. Spencer stood up once Shalon stopped crying. He helped her to her feet and led her to the living room sofa. Shalon sat on the sofa in silence. Spencer cleaned up the broken glass and tried to get the house back in order. When he was finished, he sat next to Shalon. She grabbed his hand. "Thank you. You are a wonderful friend," she told him as she laid her head on his shoulder. "You don't have to thank me. I will always be here for you." "Spencer—" she began "Yes?" he answered. "Pray for me," she finished. "I surely will," he said before going into prayer. "Lord, I come to You on behalf of my friend, my sister in You. She is hurting right now but I know she can find comfort in You. I ask that You heal her broken heart and give her strength to forgive. Let her remember that she can turn to You for anything and no substance can fill the void like You can. Give her peace so that she can rest tonight. In Jesus name I pray. Amen." Shalon kissed the front of his hand and drifted off to sleep.

Chapter 5

Shalon woke up to the sun shining in her face from the living room window. Her eyes were sensitive to the light so she squinted as she lifted herself up on the sofa. Lady was curled up under her and Spencer was on the other sofa, asleep. She has the worse headache and can barely remember why Spencer is there. She slowly stood up and walked to her front door to let Lady out. As she returned to the living room, she was greeted by Spencer who was stretching. "Good Morning. How are you feeling?" "I feel like I've been hit by a bus," she said as she sat back down. "I am pretty sure you do," he said, watching her rub her temples. "What happened last night?" she asked. "You came to the church drunk as all get out. I brought you home," He answered. Shalon, shocked and ashamed of her actions, covered her face with her hands. "Omigod! Are you serious?" she screamed into her hands. She looked at Spencer who was shaking his head yes. "Did anybody see me? Like, did I go inside the church? Was Pastor there? And if so, what did he say?" she bombarded him with questions. "I am so embarrassed!" she continued. "Calm down. No one saw you. You called me to let me know you were outside and I came out and brought you home," he assured her. "Thank God!" she heaved a sigh of relief. "Thank you, Spencer, for bringing me home. I can't believe I allowed myself to get so impaired, and then had the nerve to drive." "It definitely wasn't smart of you. But I am thankful you are safe!" he told her. "Did I pour my heart out to why I was out of character?" she asked. He shook his head yes. "You did. I am sorry you are going through this. However, I am more than confident that you will get through this. The both of you." "I don't know, Spencer, but I hope so," she said not really knowing what the outcome will be.

The two grabbed a quick breakfast from Mrs. Helen's Place and then headed to the church so that Shalon could get her car. There were a few other cars in the parking lot, one belonging to Rodney. "What is he doing here?" she asked out loud. "I don't know, maybe he saw your car and went inside to look for you," Spencer answered trying to make sense out of it. Rodney barely comes to church, so it's very out the ordinary for him to be here especially on a Saturday. "He probably wants to talk to you." "Well, he can save his breath! I don't want to hear anything he has to say right now," Shalon said, crossing her arms over her chest. "That's understandable," Spencer said, and then opened his door to get out of his car. He walked over to the passenger side to open the door for Shalon. Shalon got out and gave him a hug and thanked him once again for being a good friend. Spencer walked Shalon to her car and as he was opening the door for her, Rodney walked out of the church. Shalon and Spencer looked at each other, and then at Rodney. Rodney wasn't pleased to see Shalon with Spencer. Rodney ran up to them both and pushed Spencer, and then punched him in the face. "Rodney, stop!" Shalon shouted trying to pull Rodney away from Spencer. "You're going to cause a scene!" Shalon said, feeling embarrassed by Rodney's actions. "I can handle it from here, bruh," Rodney told Spencer dismissing him. Spencer shook his head with his jaws and fists clenched ready to charge back at Rodney. "Spencer, don't," Shalon said. Spencer glanced at Shalon, she nodded her head that he should leave. "Very well. I will see you tomorrow, Shalon. Great day, Rodney." Spencer left the two alone. Shalon watched Spencer get into his car and drive away. "You didn't have to do that!" Shalon said of Rodney assaulting Spencer. "He is overstepping his boundaries. I will not let a man disrespect me. He's lucky I didn't concrete to pavement his face." "Are you serious? He has been nothing but a friend to me," Shalon said, thrown off by Rodney's statement. "Friend, church member, brother, whatever! He's still a man at the end of the day. He might think this is the perfect opportunity to prey on your weakness," Rodney explained. "He's not even like that," Shalon told him. "Well, then he's gay!" Rodney said, putting his hands up and shrugging his shoulders. Shalon frowned at Rodney's comment. "Enough of this! Why are you here?" she asked. "I came here to talk to Bishop Goodwin. I scheduled us to have marriage counseling," he informed her. "What did you tell him?" "I told him I want my marriage. Shalon, baby, I love you. I don't want to lose you. I know I hurt you and I am a fool for doing so. Let's work this out. I promise I will never do this to you again," he said sincerely. Shalon looked away and shook her head no. She sucked her teeth, and then looked up to the sky as tears filled her eyes. "Baby, let's go through counseling. Let's make this work," he begged. "I need time, Rodney. I need time," she said as she got into her car. "Shalon—" Shalon shut her door before he could say anything else and started up her car and pulled off. Rodney put his hands on top of his head and kicked the ground as he watched Shalon drive away.

Shalon went home and cleaned the house from top to bottom. Then she took a shower and got dressed. Once she got settled, she kneeled beside her bed and prayed. She prayed for guidance and for her heart not to be hardened. After praying, she lounged on the chaise in her bedroom with a cup of tea and began to read a women's daily devotional book. The passage for today spoke on forgiveness with supporting scriptures from Ephesians 4:31-32, 'Let all bitterness, and wrath, and anger, and clamour, and evil speaking, be put away from you, with all malice:And be ye kind one to another, tenderhearted, forgiving one another, even as God for Christ's sake hath forgiven you.' Shalon closed the book while shaking her head. "I hear You, Lord, but it's so hard," she said. Her cell phone started ringing. *It's probably Rodney,* she thought. She grabbed her phone and to her surprise, it was her pastor. Hesitant to answer, she watched it ring. She finally answered the call. "Hello." "Shalon, this is your pastor. How are you?" "Hi, Bishop, I am fine. How are you?" "I am great! Thanks for asking. I know you are probably wondering why I've called. I need your assistance here at the church. Can you come in as soon as possible?" *What does he need help with?* she thought, not wanting to ask him. Instead, she agreed to come without question. "Sure, Bishop, I am on my way." "Thank you, Shalon! I will see you soon," Bishop

Goodwin said, and then hung up. Still confused as to what he needs help with, she made her way over to the church. When she got there, she went to the administrative assistant's desk in front of Bishop Goodwin's office. "Hi, Shalon!" the administrative assistant, Tara, greeted her. "Hi, Tara! I am here to see Bishop." "Okay. One moment." Tara pressed the intercom system to Bishop Goodwin's office. "Bishop, Shalon Harris is here to see you." "Great! Send her in. Thank You," he responded. "Go ahead in, Shalon." Tara smiled opening the door for Shalon. Shalon smiled back and entered Bishop's office. When she entered, she saw Rodney sitting in a chair in front of Bishop's desk. Bishop Goodwin got up from his desk and gave Shalon a hug. "What's going on?" she asked. "Have a seat, Shalon." Bishop Goodwin directed her. Shalon looked at Rodney who was looking pitiful as she sat down. "So you set me up, Bishop," she said as Bishop sat down in his chair. Bishop Goodwin put his elbows on his desk with his hands clasped together under his chin. He chuckled at her remark. "It may seem that way. However, I do need your assistance. I need you here for your husband. He asked for my help, but I can't help him without you." Bishop Goodwin opened up a notebook and began to write in it. "Rodney shared his wrongdoings with me and he also expressed how he wants to fix it. Before we get started, I must ask you, Shalon. Do you want to work on saving your marriage?" "I still love him, that hasn't changed. I wish more than anything that this was a bad dream. My heart still wants this man but my mind can't erase the image," Shalon said. "Look at him and tell him that," Bishop Goodwin instructed." Shalon turned to Rodney to face him. "I love you, Rodney. I still want to be with you, but it's hard to move passed this." "I love you, too, Shalon! And I am willing to put in the work so that we can move passed this." "Rodney, what did you get out of Shalon's statement?" Bishop Goodwin asked. "That she loves me but can't get over what I've done." "And Shalon, what did you get out of Rodney's statement?" "That he loves me and that he will do whatever to make it right," Shalon answered. "So we are all in agreement that you both love each other and want to be together. That brings me back to this question: Shalon, are you willing to work on your marriage?" Bishop Goodwin waited on Shalon to respond. "Yes," she finally answered. "Rodney, do you truly want to work on your marriage? Are you willing to turn away from those actions that brought you here?" Bishop questioned. "Yes, sir, more than anything. On my life, I will never betray her again," Rodney responded. "Well then, let us pray and begin this road to recovery," Bishop said before he went into prayer. After the counseling session, the couple agreed to meet with the Bishop twice a week until they work through everything. Shalon still wasn't ready for Rodney to come home. To give her space and time that she requested, he went back to the hotel he occupied the night before.

***

"Hi, Spencer." Shalon welcomed him as he entered the church. It is Sunday morning and the praise team and musicians were meeting up to pray and go over final selections before Sunday morning service began. Shalon and Spencer were the first to arrive so it gave them a little time to catch up. "I am so sorry about yesterday," Shalon said, looking at the bruising on his face. "You don't have to apologize. How is everything going with you?" Spencer asked. "Just taking it day by day," she responded. "That's a start. I will continue to pray for you," he said, giving her hand a squeeze. "Thank you," she smiled. The other members of the praise team entered in. They all greeted one another and immediately went into prayer. "Lord, we just thank You for bringing us here one more time to glorify You. In your word, it says that everything that has breath should praise Your name and to be obedient to Your word, we will cry out Hallelujah. Let us set our flesh aside and be lead by Your spirit as we lead the congregation into praise and worship. Let Your glory fall into this place. We pray that healing, deliverance, and lives are saved today. Bless our pastor as he brings forth Your word to bless us. We love You and we thank You," Spencer led the group in prayer. "Amen," they all said in unison. As the musicians and other members of the praise team headed to the sanctuary, Shalon stayed behind. She wanted to pray alone. "Lord, in spite of what's going on in my life, You are still a mighty God. I know that if You brought me to it, You will bring me through it. As mentioned earlier by Spencer, let me set my flesh aside so I can praise You with all of me. I still trust You. Amen."

Near the end of service, Bishop Goodwin invited those who wanted prayer to come forth. During this time the praise team is to be on assignment, so they entered onto the pulpit and begin to softly sing 'It's Not Over (When God is In It)' by Israel & New Breed featuring James Fortune. Shalon closed her eyes and felt every word of the song. When she opened her eyes, she saw Rodney get up from the back pew and walk down the aisle to the altar. She was surprised to see him because she didn't know he was in attendance. Shalon kept singing as she watched as a minister smeared anointing oil on Rodney's forehead. Rodney was signaled by an altar worker to go to Bishop Goodwin. Bishop Goodwin instructed Rodney to raise his hands and asked him privately his prayer request. Rodney told Bishop Goodwin that he wanted to repent and that he wanted his wife. "Glory God!" Bishop Goodwin said out loud with excitement, he prayed over Rodney. "Because you boldly walked up here seeking Him, He said you are forgiven!" Bishop Goodwin announced. Rodney fell to his knees in worship. "Shalon, come be with your husband," Bishop instructed. Shalon went down to the altar and kneeled beside Rodney and rubbed his back. Rodney looked up at Shalon with tears in his eyes. She stood up and helped him to his feet. "I am sorry. I will make this right, even if it takes forever," Rodney said, holding his wife's waist. Shalon feeling overwhelmed with emotions, tears began to roll down her cheeks. She held her husband's face and wiped his tears. "Because we serve a forgiving God and he has forgiven you, I, too, forgive you. I love you and want us to make this work." The two hugged and the church broke out in praise.

No Longer Her

Chapter 1

I can't believe I have gotten myself in this situation again, Lexi thought as she pried the arm of a sleeping man off her, whom she met the night before at a club that she currently works at. She slowly and quietly got out of the bed and gathered her things. Lexi went to the bathroom to freshen up. Thoughts of last night swarming through her head. The loud music, crowded club, clouds of smoke, and eyes of lustful men. Lexi is an exotic dancer at a popular gentlemen's club in her area. Her original plan was to dance for a few months to supplement her low paying part time job until she found something full time. However, five years has passed and she hasn't left. Lexi looked at herself in the mirror. Mascara ruined, faded lipstick, and tangled hair. An image that has become all too familiar to her. Lexi, short for Alexis, is an attractive woman. Some would say breath-taking. She has a statuesque frame standing at about 5'8, weighing around 145. Her caramel complexion seemed flawless and her hair rested below her shoulders. Her best asset would have to be her eyes. They were bright and inviting. One can barely tell that those eyes are usually filled with tears. Lexi has been on her own since she was 16. Her home life was tough growing up. Her father has been incarcerated since she was 13 years old. When Lexi was 13 her mother's then boyfriend took her innocence. She immediately told her mother after it happen but her mother didn't want to believe it. And she told Lexi to never speak on the situation again. But this was not something Lexi could pretend didn't happen, especially since it became an ongoing thing. It got so bad that Lexi had thoughts of suicide. The fear of a grown man forcing himself on her and threatening to kill her if she told became unbearable. Lexi became pregnant and when her mother asked who fathered the child, she became enraged at Lexi's response that she beat Lexi causing her to miscarry. Lexi ran away and went to a friend's house. While there, she called her father. Her father picked her up and she told him everything. Her father, full of anger, went to her mother's house with a loaded pistol and killed both her mother and mother's boyfriend. After her father was convicted of both murders, Lexi was ordered by the state to stay with her paternal grandparents. Her grandparents were very strict and over protective. Which was very understandable, but Lexi was rebellious and couldn't stand living under their firm hand. So she left home and got a part time job working at one of the local grocery stores. She lived couch to couch until she was 18 and got her first apartment. Tired of living paycheck to paycheck and barely making her rent payments, she decided to become an exotic dancer. This lifestyle has led Lexi to do things she said she would never do—the occasional sleeping around with men if the price is right, depending on drugs to numb the pain and consuming alcohol to forget it all. Lexi looked in the mirror one final time and took a long deep breath. She walked out of the bathroom and was a little startled when she saw the once sleeping man sitting up in bed, touching his manhood while smiling at her. "Hey, Angel Eyes, ready for round two?" he said. "No!" she replied with disgust. "Why not? We still have a couple hours before check out. Come call me daddy again," he continued. "Have fun by yourself! I am out of here," Lexi said as she walked towards the door to leave. As she walked out the door, the man called her name. She turned and glanced at him, he was winking his eye and blowing kisses. Lexi frowned and walked out the door. "Ughhh! I can't do this anymore," she said out loud to herself. Lexi walked out the hotel building realizing she didn't drive there. Letting out a sigh, she pulled out her cell phone and called her best friend of ten years, Carla. "Hey, trick!" Carla answered. "Good morning to you, too!" Lexi responded. Carla laughed and said, "I love youuuu! What's up?" "Girl I need you to come get me at Bell Inn," Lexi told her friend. "Bell Inn? Really, Lexi?" Carla said a little disappointed. This is not the first time she has picked her friend up from a hotel. She knows the lifestyle her friend lives and doesn't agree with it but loves her the same. "I am on my way, hon," Carla assured Lexi. "Thanks! Love you lots. Call me when you are here," Lexi said to Carla before ending the phone call. Lexi didn't want to wait for Carla in front of the hotel or risk coming back in contact with the man she spent her night with, so she decided to sit at a bus stop nearby. While sitting at the bus stop, Lexi's mind began to wander to her childhood and her now adulthood. *Why do I do these things? I do not want to live like this anymore. This is not how I envisioned my life to be,* she thought. She looked up to the sky and began to pray. "God, I don't know what to say. I haven't prayed in so long, but I feel like I need to say something. I am so disgusted with myself. I cannot live like this anymore. Please help me." Before she could say Amen, Carla pulled up to the bus stop and blew her horn. Lexi immediately got up and entered Carla's car. "Hey, I tried to call," Carla told Lexi. Lexi looked down at her phone and saw Carla's two missed calls. "Is everything OK?" Carla continued. "Yes, everything is fine. I didn't realize I still had my phone on silent," Lexi replied. Lexi looked at Carla. *Carla is so well put together,* she thought. Carla is average build and height with a beautiful chocolate complexion and long curly hair that she wears in its natural state. She has a pretty smile and dimple. She is so smart graduating at the top of her class with a degree in Biology. Carla wants to continue her education and become a doctor. Some wonder how two different personalities as Lexi and Carla managed to stay friends this long. "Why are you staring at me?" Carla said. "You are so weird!" Carla finished jokingly. "I was looking at you, thinking I wanna be just like you when I grow up!" Lexi said in her best child's voice. They both began to laugh. "Where is your car? Is it still at the club?" Carla asked. "No, I rode with another dancer last night," Lexi responded. "Oh, OK! So y'all got a carpooling system going on now?" Carla said, teasing her friend. "No!" Lexi managed to say while laughing. Carla pulled up to Lexi's apartment complex and both girls got out the car and went inside Lexi's apartment. Glad to be home, Lexi rushed to her bathroom to take a shower. Carla made herself at home as usual and turned on Lexi's television. Wow! *This is new!* Carla thought taking in the view of the new 70 inch flat screen in Lexi's living room. Lexi's apartment is nicely furnished. A white leather sectional sofa with red and black decorative pillows, a black, white, and red area rug with abstract designs, and paintings on the wall gave Lexi's living room a modern fresh look. This girl has great style and taste Carla admired of her friends nice home. Carla continued to channel surf until Lexi was done getting herself cleaned up. "Ahhhh, I feel so much better!" Lexi said, feeling rejuvenated as she entered her living room wearing a white tank top and pink shorts with her hair in a bun. She plopped on the sofa next to Carla. "Finally!" Carla said, pushing her friend playfully. "You make it seem like I was gone for hours!" Lexi said, pushing Carla back. "Well, at least you take time to wash your butt," Carla said jokingly. "Omigod!" Lexi shrieked, "Of course! My lady parts, too!" Both girls laughed and joked for a little while longer. Then Carla directed the conversation to a church she has recently been visiting. "So, Lexi, I have been visiting a church for a few weeks now," Carla began, "it's awesome there! The music is great and the word delivered is always powerful. And best of all, the Spirit is thick in that place." Carla lit up. Speaking of this church, Lexi could tell Carla enjoyed the service. This, in turn, made her very interested. "Really?" Lexi asked wanting to know more. "Yes! And the members there are very welcoming! The pastor and his wife even personally greets every visitor. They are very nice," Carla continued. "I really think you should come with me this Sunday," Carla insisted. "I haven't been to a church in years!" Lexi said. "I must admit I am kind of nervous," Lexi admitted.

"I am not living right and I don't wanna be in church with all my dirt," Lexi finished, looking down rubbing her hands. Carla grabbed Lexi's hands and held them. "You will be fine. No one is perfect; everyone has fallen short of the glory. But that doesn't mean you can't recover from it. This is the perfect time to go, when you are a mess. You just got to allow him to make you clean," Carla assured her friend. "This is why you are my best friend. You always tell me what I need to hear," Lexi said, feeling a little better about visiting this church. "Exactly, I have no problems telling you what you need to hear, like let's go shopping because none of your clothes are church friendly!" Carla teased. "Hey! What happened to *come as you are?*" Lexi challenged. "By the way, I do have 'church friendly' clothes, thank you very much," Lexi said with her hands on her hips doing the sister girl neck roll. "Riiiight, shopping trip it is!" Carla announced. Once again the ladies had their moments of laughter. They decided that they would meet up later during the week to do a little shopping.

Chapter 2

A few days has passed and Sunday is finally here. Lexi was giving herself a final spin looking into the mirror. She wore her hair down with loose curls and put her makeup on perfectly. She picked out a black knee length pencil skirt and a tan short sleeved blouse to wear. A lover of high heels she put on her favorite pair of black designer pumps. "Well alright now! Look at you with your Sunday best on," Carla said as she entered Lexi's bedroom. "Ha Ha! This is definitely not my Sunday's best, but if I do say so myself, I clean up pretty nice when I want to," Lexi responded. "This is true!" Carla replied. "Oh my, look at the time! We need to be heading out if we want to make it to service on time," Carla told Lexi. "Grab your Bible and let's go," Carla said as she grabbed her purse and headed to the living room. "Uhhh, Bible? I don't have one. Of all things, I cannot believe I don't own a Bible!" Lexi said, feeling a little embarrassed. "It's okay! We will make sure to get you one later. Good thing we are living in a world where there is an app for everything. Just download a Bible app on your phone," Carla told Lexi as they walked out of Lexi's apartment. *I can't believe I don't have a Bible! I am more messed up than I thought!* Lexi thought to herself as she entered the passenger side of Carla's car. On the ride to the church, Carla played gospel music. It reminded Lexi of the times her grandmother would play gospel music really loud on Saturday mornings as she cooked and cleaned. "We are here!" Carla informed Lexi as they pulled up to the church. "Kingdom Life Ministries" Lexi read the name of the church on the sign. "Why do I want to leave all of sudden, like I just don't need to go in there?" Lexi asked Carla. "Because the devil is busy, and he wants to keep you from a word you may need to hear. But not today, Devil! Not today!" Carla said. "Well, it must be a powerful word that the enemy doesn't want me to hear, because I am reminded of all my wrongdoings and don't want to feel out of place around all these church folks," Lexi told Carla as they walked up to the church doors. "Don't worry, honey! I really believe you will enjoy it here," Carla said before they were greeted by an usher. "Good morning, ladies! My name is Sister Anita Davis, and on behalf of our pastor, Bishop Eugene, and First Lady Valerie Goodwin, I would like to welcome you to Kingdom Life Ministries!" the usher said, welcoming them in with a warm smile and hug. "It's good to have you back, Carla, and I am glad you brought a friend." The usher gave the ladies a church bulletin, a visitors card, and led them into the sanctuary to be seated. Once inside the sanctuary, the ladies were welcomed by more members of the church. "Wow, is it just me or are these people overfriendly?" Lexi whispered to Carla. "Girl, chill! I told you the members here are very welcoming!" Carla laughed. An older gentleman walked up to the pulpit and asked the congregation to stand as he led prayer and read a scripture. Afterwards the praise and worship service began. "You are going to love the music here! This is not your typical type of 'church music' that your Granny grew up on!" Carla insisted. The praise team entered the pulpit. They consist of six vocalist and five musicians who were dressed very colorful and youthful. The praise leader gave a testimony on how good God has been to him, gave the musicians their cue and it was on from there. The first strum of the bass guitar literally set the tone, and then came the drums, and the keyboard. It almost felt as if it was a rock concert mixed with hip hop and r&b, but still managed to have a gospel sound. It was definitely a sound Lexi had never heard in church before. Everyone was up on their feet clapping, singing, and dancing. The praise turned into worship, and all you could see were saints with their hands up and heads back, proclaiming their love for the Lord. Lexi began to feel some type of way, almost uncomfortable. She glanced over at Carla who had tears in her eyes as she was in deep worship. Lexi heard the praise leader say to the congregation, "Just open your mouth and tell Him you love him you owe Him the fruit of your lips." Lexi closed her eyes so she wouldn't be distracted by watching the others as they worshipped. With her eyes closed and hands clasped, she began to pray: "God I am not used to praising and worshipping You. I am not even sure if I am praying to You correctly. But I do know I want to change my life. Please show me how. Amen." As Lexi opened her eyes, she noticed a man entered the pulpit. *He must be the pastor of the church,* she thought. He was middle aged, tall, and attractive to the eye. His demeanor was calm and warm. He held his bible and walked up to the podium. "Our Savior is in this place, saints! He deserves all your praise and worship. Just opening your mouth can change your situation. You don't have to leave here the same way you came in." The pastor began to pray, and then guided the congregation to the scriptures that his sermon would come from. After the sermon, an altar call invitation was extended for those who needed prayer or wanted to make a new commitment to the Lord. Lexi sat in her seat debating if she wanted to go up to the altar. *I really should go up for prayer,* Lexi thought to herself. *I feel like my life story is all over my face. I don't want to feel judged,* Lexi continued in thought. Lexi felt her hand being grabbed by Carla. "Let's go up for prayer," Carla said. Lexi didn't say anything; she just nodded her head and followed Carla to the front of the church. At the altar, there were a few ministers helping with prayer. An altar worker placed anointed oil on Lexi's forehead and pointed her in the direction to which minister to go to. A minister asked Lexi if she had a special prayer request. Lexi didn't want to go into detail about what she was trying to overcome, out of embarrassment. Tears began rolling down Lexi's face. The minister hugged Lexi and begin to pray for her. "Lord God, I don't know what this young lady has been through, nor do I know what she is currently going through. But because she made the first step in coming up here to seek Your grace, I pray that whatever it is she is seeking, Jesus, that You supply her every need. Let her know that she can find comfort in Your loving arms. Give her peace in her storms. Turn her pain into joy. I thank You now, Jesus, for her life! And I pray that Your grace and mercy continuously be on her. Amen." "Amen," Lexi said once the minister was done praying for her. The minister hugged Lexi once more. Lexi turned around to walk back to her seat, but before she could, the pastor of the church motioned for an altar worker to bring her to him. Once Lexi was standing in front of him, he told her that her past doesn't define her future and he prayed over her as well. Tears in her eyes, Lexi walked back to her seat where Carla met her with a hug. Altar call came to an end and soon service was being dismissed. After service, the members and visitors hugged one another and socialized. "Hi! I am so glad you came to worship with us today! How are you?" the first lady of the church said to Lexi with a big smile and extended a hug to her. "I am well! Thank you for asking," Lexi responded, "I really enjoyed service." As the two were talking, the pastor came and joined in their conversation. He extended his hand out to shake Lexi's hand. "Hello, I am Bishop Goodwin. How are you?" "I am well! I was just telling your beautiful wife how much I enjoyed service," Lexi told the pastor. "Well, good! I am glad you enjoyed and I hope to see you again soon!" Bishop Goodwin said with a big smile. "You will see her again, I promise!" Carla said, joining the three. "Carla! It's good to see you!" "Yes, it is! Thanks for joining us again and bringing a friend." The pastor and first lady said, acknowledging Carla. The four chatted a little more, and then the pastor introduced Lexi and Carla to the praise team and musicians since they were nearby. "You all sound amazing!" Carla told the music department. "Thank you!" they all said in unison. Lexi noticed that one of the praise team members was looking at her as if she knew her. "Hi, Lexi! I am Shalon," the member who was looking at her strangely finally spoke. "Hi, Shalon, nice to meet you," Lexi greeted her. "You look so familiar, have we met before?" Shalon asked. "I don't think so," Lexi responded. After a little more chatting of how they may know each other—for instance, old neighborhood, high school, college, etc.—they realized that they have never met. "I guess I have one of those faces, I heard everyone has a twin somewhere," Lexi said with a laugh. Shalon looked at her once more still trying to figure out where she knew Lexi from. Shalon responded, "Yeah, you are right! Well, it was nice meeting you!" Carla and Lexi told everyone goodbye and left the church.

As the ladies walked to Carla's car, other members of the church who were in the parking lot waved good-bye to them. The ladies waved back. Once in the car the ladies began to talk about the service. "Soooo, what did you think?" Carla asked. "It was everything you said it would be!" Lexi said. "It was so live and the message really spoke to me! Thanks for inviting me."

Lexi told her friend. "I knew you would like it," Carla said, smiling. "Carla, so what is Shalon like? I mean, have you two spoken?" Lexi asked. "Uhm, I really don't know her to say. We have only spoke in passing. She seems nice. Why do you ask?" Carla answered. "I was just wondering. I might just be overanalyzing things, but she was somewhat giving me the stank eye," Lexi explained. "She kept trying to figure where she knows my face from, but I have never seen her before," Lexi finished. "Umm… I don't know. I wouldn't read too much into it but I will do a little research on her," Carla said as she pulled up to a soul food restaurant where they will have lunch. "Ooh, I love this place! They have the best fried catfish and white beans!" Lexi's attention switched to the restaurant called Mrs. Helen's Place. "I know right! I been thinking about the greens and mac-n-cheese served here all week!" Carla said as they got out of her car to head inside the eatery. Once inside, the ladies were seated by the hostess. "Your waiter will be with you soon!" the hostess told them with a smile while handing them a menu. "Thank you!" the ladies said in unison. "I don't even need to look at the menu, I already know what I want!" Lexi said. "Exactly!" Carla agreed. "Hello, ladies! My name is Reese and I will be your waiter today." The waiter greeted them as he placed a complimentary basket of biscuits and cornbread on their table. "Hi, Reese! Those look great!" Carla greeted the waiter and looked at the basket in awe. "Can I start you two off with a drink while you look at the menu?" Reese asked. "Actually, we are ready to order," Lexi told him. "Great! What can I get you?" Reese asked pulling out his pen and notepad to take their order. "I will have the fried catfish with white beans and coleslaw meal, and fruit tea to drink, please," Lexi placed her order. "And I will have fried chicken with turnip greens, and mac-n-cheese, with a sweet tea to drink," Carla told the waiter. "Oh, and can you add meatloaf and a small side of mashed potatoes with gravy," Carla added to her order. "Sure!" Reese said as he jotted their orders on his notepad. "I will be back with your orders soon," he informed the ladies before leaving their table. "Somebody is hungry!" Lexi said, teasing her friend. "Girl, this is my only cheat day out of the week. So I gotta get it in!" Carla said. "I must say, I can really tell you have been eating right and working out. You look great! So enjoy your cheat day, honey!" Lexi said, applauding Carla's dedication to being fit and healthy. "Thank you, love!" Carla said after the compliment. Lexi was looking around the restaurant when she noticed at the entrance a young man walking in. He is very pleasing to the eye. Tall, dark skinned, clean cut goatee, and well dressed. "Doesn't that guy play the keyboard at Kingdom Life Ministries?" Lexi asked Carla motioning her to look at the guy. "Yes, he does! That's Joc," Carla said, looking over at him. Joc sees the women looking at him and realized that they are visitors from church. He waved and made his way over to their table. "Hey!" he greeted the ladies. "Hi!" the ladies said together. "It's good to see you both again!" he told them. "Likewise," Carla said. "Well, I just came in here to order some banana pudding. It's almost as good as my Momma's," he said, grinning. "I have never tried it from here, I am gonna have to order some for dessert," Lexi told him. "Me, too!" Carla chimed in. "Yes, definitely do that. You will love it!" he told them. Joc made eye contact with Lexi. "Lexi, right?" he asked. "Yes," she said, starting to blush at him remembering her name from when she was introduced earlier. "I am Joc. I don't think we actually spoke earlier." "No, we didn't" Lexi responded. "Hopefully, we can change that," Joc told Lexi. Lexi began to twirl a strand of hair with her head cocked to the side. She smiled at Joc and replied, "You should call me sometime. What is your number?" she reached into her purse to pull out her cell phone. Joc recited his number to Lexi. As he did this, Lexi dialed the number on her phone. Joc's phone began to ring. "Save my number," she told him. "Will do!" he said and just then, the waiter came back to the table with the ladies' food and drinks. "Enjoy your meal, ladies, and please let me know if you need something else," the waiter said as he left their table. "Well, I hope to talk to you soon, Lexi, and I hope to see you both at church again. I am gonna let you two get to your meals now. Enjoy the rest of your day," Joc stated. The ladies told him bye and watched as he picked up his order and left the restaurant. "Ooh girl! What was that about?" Carla said to her friend sipping her ice tea. Lexi smiled at her friend and said, "Honey, let's blessed this food and eat."

Chapter 3

"Lexi! You're up next," the club owner, Mac, shouted through the dressing room door. "OK! I'll be out in a sec!" she answered. She looked at herself in the mirror one last time. She had on a gold bra bedazzled in rhinestones with a matching thong and six-inch heels. She had on lots of makeup on and wore her hair bone straight. She picked up two shot glasses filled with tequila and drank both, back to back. As she walked to the dressing room door to leave out, a dancer by the name of Jade walked in. "Heeey, Ma! It's poppin' out there tonight," the dancer told Lexi. "Yasss, that's wassup!" Lexi responded. "Here, hit this before you go," Jade said, handing Lexi a joint. "It's that good-good," Jade said as she watched Lexi take a pull off the joint. Lexi began to cough. "Damn!" Lexi began before coughing again. Jade laughed and said, "I told you it was that good-good!" "Girl, I am not fooling with you tonight, you got me in here choking and shit," Lexi laughed as she walked out the dressing room. "Alright, gentlemen! We got another bombshell coming to the stage, so keep those dollars out and make it rain for Angel Eyes!" the d.j. announced, introducing Lexi by her stage name. Lexi walked out on the stage slowly and seductively until she got to the end of the stage. She began to dance, which consisted of a slow sensual floor and pole routine. She climbed up the pole and swung around it, and then swirled down the pole ending in a split. She walked to the edge of the stage and turned around so that her back is facing the audience. She slowly bent over and rolled her hips "Yes, Baby!" "Ooh, weee!" "Yeaaaa" Lexi heard the crowd say as she danced. As her routine came to an end, she began to flirt with some of the gentlemen near the front of the stage, by blowing kisses and touching some of their faces. "Give it up for Angel Eyes! She did her thang," the d.j. said as Lexi collected her tips. Lexi left the stage and was headed back to the dressing room. "Hey, Lexi!" Mac approached her. "What?" Lexi asked. "Why must all you heffas have attitudes?" Mac asked with a cigar hanging out his mouth. "Whatever, I don't have an attitude. What do you need?" Lexi asked becoming annoyed. "Your little friend is here and he has requested a private dance," the club owner said, pointing up to the VIP section. Lately, there has been a well-suited man coming into the club. He always requests Lexi and tips her very well. "Thanks for letting me know," Lexi thanked Mac. She grabbed a drink from the bar and made her way to the VIP section. She spotted the gentleman sitting on a sofa, having a drink. The gentleman wore a dark designer suit, with a lattice patterned tie, and Italian leather shoes. He is in his early 30s, has an athletic build, and stands around 6'0 feet tall. He's light skinned with dark eyes and a short dark hair cut. He's a few shades lighter than what Lexi likes, but she found him to be very attractive. "Hello, beautiful!" he stood up to greet her. She smiled and gave him a hug. "I have a present for you," the gentleman said as he pulled out twenty 100 dollar bills out of his coat pocket. Lexi smiled and finished the drink that was in her hand, straddled the gentlemen, and began to give him a lap dance.

***

Beep beep beep! The alarm clock on Lexi's phone went off. Lexi still half way sleep picked up her phone to silence the alarm. She re-positioned herself in her bed to get back comfy. Ring Ring Ring! "You have got to be freakin' kidding me!" Lexi yelled as she looked at the incoming call on her cell phone. "Hello!" Lexi answered in an annoyed voice. "Hey, Lexi! Did I call you at a bad time?" the voice said on the other end. "Who is this?" Lexi asked. "Joc," the voice answered. Lexi set up in her bed and cleared her throat. "Hi, Joc." "Did I reach you at a bad time?" he asked again. "I can call you back later," he said.

"No, no. It's not a bad time," Lexi quickly said. "You sound as if you were asleep," Joc said. "My alarm went off right before you called, so I haven't been awake long," she told him. "Late sleeper I see," Joc stated being that it was 11:30 a.m. "Only when I work at night," she told him. "That's cool. I understand how that goes. I am all too familiar with the night shift," Joc said. "You work nights, too?" Lexi asked. "Nah, not anymore. I used to for many years, though," he answered. "So how have you been?" Joc asked Lexi. "I have been good!" she answered. "I am glad to hear from you!" she told him. "For a minute I thought you forgot about me. You didn't know who I was when you picked up the phone. Talking about 'Who is this?'" Joc said, jokingly. "I am sorry about that, I know that had to sound super rude," she apologized. "It's cool," he assured her. They talked on the phone for about an hour and decided to meet up later that evening for dinner.

After her phone conversation with Joc, Lexi got up to tidy up her home. She began by starting a load of laundry. She grabbed her bag with her garments that she performed in last night so that they could be washed. The events of last night replayed in her head. She had a good night pay wise. She brought home close to $3000. Most of it was from her generous tipper in VIP. She has danced for him several times. The first couple of times was strictly that—just dancing. Then one night he offered Lexi a pretty coin she couldn't refuse. So now every time she sees him she gives him a little extra and he compensates her well. Lexi began to feel disgusted with herself, as the thoughts of the gentleman having his way with her crossed her mind. I can't keep allowing myself to do this! She began to think about what Bishop Goodwin told her when she went up for prayer. That her past doesn't define her future. She stopped what she was doing and dropped to her knees. Lexi began to pray and as she prayed, she also repented. And in that moment, she decided she was not going to dance and sell her body for money again.

***

Lexi pulled up to an upscale Asian restaurant to meet Joc for dinner. The valet opened her door to let her out and to park her car. She thanked the valet for his services and entered the restaurant. The host at the door welcomed Lexi in and asked her what name was her reservation under. Joc told Lexi earlier that it would be under Joc D. party of two. She relayed the information to the host. "Yes! Your party is waiting for you now. Follow me," the host told Lexi and walked her to the table where Joc was sitting. Joc's eyes lit up once he saw Lexi. She looked stunning. She wore a black dress and black peep toe heels. She wore her hair in its big curly natural state mainly because she sweated her bone straight style out last night at the club. She didn't overdo her makeup, but she did decide to wear a bold matte plum shade lipstick. She was pleased with the sight of him as well. He had on a light blue button-down shirt, a navy vest, a burgundy and white gingham style tie, and dark blue straight leg jeans. Joc stood up and gave her a hug, and then pulled out her chair for Lexi to be seated. "Wow, this place looks nice," Lexi said as she was seated. "Yeah, I have heard great reviews about this place," Joc said as he sat down. "You look beautiful, by the way," he complimented her. "Thank you! You are lookin' pretty nice yourself!" Lexi complimented back. "Yeah, yeah, I tend to clean up pretty nice," Joc said, rubbing his hand on his goatee. They both laughed at his humorous tone. *Mmm, he has a beautiful smile,* Lexi thought to herself admiring his straight white teeth. Their waitress approached their table and introduced herself. She gave them both menus and told them about their house special for that night. Lexi and Joc needed time to look over the dinner menu but went ahead a placed their drink order. Lexi was looking at the different types of wines and ordered the Riesling. Joc ordered sparkling water with lime. "Not a wine drinker?" she asked. "Nah. I had to leave all that alone. I use to be a hardcore drinker. Anything with alcohol in it I would drink like water! I don't have a taste for it anymore," he informed her. "Wow, okay. That's cool. I hope it doesn't offend you that I ordered wine," Lexi told him. "No, no, no. It doesn't bother me," he assured her. As the night went on, the two conversed quite a bit. They shared their likes and dislikes, hobbies, favorite things to do, and upbringings. In the beginning, Lexi didn't go into full detail about her childhood but she did mention that she was raised by her grandparents. Joc shared that he was born and raised here in town by his single mother. His mother struggled to make ends meet working a minimum wage job and receiving welfare. So as a teen, he did what everyone else in his environment did. He began hustling, pushing drugs for the major drug dealers until he became a major drug dealer himself. He also shared that a tragic incident caused him to change his whole life. So now he travels doing a lot of motivational speaking and mentors young boys and men in the community. Lexi was in awe of his story that it compelled her to share a little more about her past. She really hasn't opened up to too many people about her childhood. That's a part of her life she rather forget. However, she felt so comfortable with Joc that she explained why she was raised by her grandparents. Feeling a little uneasy after letting him in on her tumultuous past, she felt like she needed to call it a night. "I think I should get going now." "Already? Is everything okay?" he asked after she abruptly wanted to end their date. "Everything's fine. It's just getting kind of late," she told him. "Yeah, you're right. It is getting kind of late. Time flies when you are having fun," he said as he signaled the waitress for their check. Joc paid for their check and left a tip for the waitress. He then waited with Lexi as the valet went to get her car. "Thanks for dinner tonight. I really enjoyed your company," Lexi told Joc. "The pleasure is all mine," he responded. "Will I see you at church again tomorrow?" he asked. "Of course," she said with a smile. The valet pulled up with Lexi's car. Lexi thanked the valet for his services and Joc tipped him. Joc opened Lexi's car door to help her inside. Before she got in, she thanked Joc once more for dinner and gave him a hug. Joc kissed her on her forehead and told her goodnight.

Chapter 4

"Hey, best friend!" Carla greeted Lexi as she opened her apartment door. "Hey, Boo!" Lexi said as she hugged her friend. Lexi decided to spend the night over at Carla's so that they could ride to church together in the morning. "So, tell me everything! From beginning to end," Carla said as she grabbed Lexi's hand and headed over to her sofa. "Well, we met up at a nice Asian restaurant downtown. The food was amazing and we had great conversation," Lexi said, reflecting on her date with Joc." "Details! I need more details, honey!" Carla shrieked. "I mean it's not much to tell, it was just dinner and conversation," Lexi started. Lexi began to think about the long hug that she and Joc shared and the sweet forehead kiss he gave her. "But I must say I felt safe in his arms, and the kiss he gave me on my forehead was everything!" Lexi finished, smiling at the thought. "Awwww, tell me more," Carla said before they both burst out laughing. "I am through with you for tonight!" Lexi said, playfully pushing Carla. The ladies called it a night and went to sleep.

Sunday morning finally came. The ladies got ready for Sunday morning service and used Lexi's car to get to the church. Once there, they once again were greeted by Sister Anita, the usher. "Praise the Lord, ladies! It's so good to see you both again." The ladies gave the usher a hug and made their way into the sanctuary. Service hadn't started yet, so most of the members were welcoming each other and socializing. First Lady Goodwin saw the girls and made her way over to speak to them. "Hello, beauties! How is everything going?" she asked as she hugged them both. "Hi! Everything is good!" Carla told her. "All is well! I am so glad to be here," Lexi responded as well. "Great! That is so wonderful to hear. I will catch up with you two after service," First Lady Goodwin told them as she hugged them again. Lexi and Carla took a seat. "Well, look who made it!" Joc said with a smile. "Good morning, Carla! Hi, Lexi," he said, extending a hug to them both. "Hi, Joc," Carla said, elbowing Lexi. Lexi elbowed her friend back and smiled at Joc. "See you after service!" Joc winked at Lexi and headed to the front of the sanctuary with the other musicians. Service had begun. Corporate prayer, scriptures read, praise and worship, and the word was delivered. Once again, another amazing service. *Wow! I have really been missing out,* Lexi thought referring to not being involved in a church. An altar call was opened for those in need of prayer, repentance, or wanting to join the church. Lexi whispered to Carla that she wanted to join the church. Carla's eyes lit up because she was having the same thoughts. They decided to join together. They walked up to the altar and informed the altar worker that they wanted to join the church. The worker relayed the message to the pastor. Bishop Goodwin was very excited. He announced to the congregation that the church has gained two new family members. Everyone in the church clapped and cheered. Bishop Goodwin prayed over both the women and asked all the members of the church to come up to the altar and welcome them. After service, a member of the welcome committee came and collected information from Lexi and Carla and asked them if they would be interested in taking part in any auxiliaries. Lexi took interest in the youth program. She was told a meeting would be taking place later in the week to plan upcoming events for the youth. After exchanging information and given a tour of the church in its entirety, Lexi and Carla returned to the sanctuary. By this time, most of the members have left. The Bishop and First Lady approached the two women. "My, my, my, praise God!" Bishop Goodwin began. "I knew it would be a matter of time before you two became family," he finished. "Yes, we are so happy and blessed to have you both here," First Lady Goodwin joined in. "Thank you for making us feel so welcomed!" Lexi thanked them. "We try our best to love on everyone," Bishop Goodwin said with a warm smile. "You two should join us for lunch," First Lady Goodwin offered. Lexi and Carla accepted the invitation. "Let me just finish a few things around here and we will be on our way," Bishop Goodwin informed them. First Lady introduced the ladies to a few more saints who were still around. Lexi noticed Joc talking to Sister Anita, the usher. She watched him give Sister Anita a hug and kiss on the cheek. Joc looked over and motioned for Lexi to come over. Lexi excused herself from Carla and the First Lady who were engaged in a conversation with a few other women. Lexi made her way over to Joc and Sister Anita. "Hey, Lexi, I want to introduce you to someone very special to me," Joc said as he looked at Sister Anita who was smiling. "This is my beautiful mother," he informed Lexi. A surprised Lexi began to notice this resemblance between the two. "Wow! I didn't know this sweet lady is your mother," Lexi said. "And I didn't know that you are the lady who has my son smiling ear to ear here lately," Sister Anita smiled and reached for Lexi's hand to give it a squeeze. Lexi blushed at hearing the impression she has left on Joc. "Well, I must say I am glad it's you!" Sister Anita said, approving of Lexi. Sister Anita gave Joc and Lexi a hug and informed them that she was about to go home and get her dinner started. After they said their goodbyes to Sister Anita, Lexi looked at Joc and gently shoved his shoulder. "Hey, hey, don't hurt me now," Joc said, playfully shielding himself. They both laughed. "Omigod! I just met your Mom! Well, technically I've met her already. But I didn't know she was your Mom!" Lexi said, covering her face. "It's all good!" Joc assured her. They locked eyes for a moment before some of the musicians walked by. They greeted Lexi and told Joc they would see him later that week at rehearsal. Shalon stopped to speak as well with the praise leader, Spencer. The conversation was mostly small talk. However, Lexi sensed some unwanted tension coming from Shalon. "So, Lexi, I heard you joined the youth committee," Shalon mentioned. "Yes, I am excited and look forward to helping out in any way I can," Lexi said, not letting Shalon's vibe intimidate her. "Well, I think you will be great and bring fresh ideas!" Spencer told Lexi. "Thank you, Spencer!" Lexi said with a nod. Lexi noticed Shalon roll her eyes. "Well, Joc, we will see you at rehearsal this week and Lexi, we will see you at the youth meeting on Friday. Enjoy the rest of your day," Spencer said before him and Shalon left. *What is up with that woman?* Lexi thought to herself about Shalon. Lexi didn't ponder on it too long because Joc immediately regained her attention. "Maybe we can see each other again soon. Hint-hint!" Joc said, hinting at another date. Lexi put her finger up to her chin and looked up to the ceiling, to imply she had to think about it. Then she playfully said, "I guess!" and then with a more serious tone, she told Joc, "I would love to see you again." Soon after, Lexi informed Joc that she and Carla would be having lunch with the Bishop and First Lady. They made plans to talk later and make arrangements for when they will go out again. Bishop Goodwin finally wrapped up everything he had to take care of. He met his wife along with Lexi and Carla at the entrance of the church. They said their final goodbyes to a couple of saints who were leaving and to Deacon Roberts who was locking the doors of the church. They made their way to the parking lot to the Bishop's black Audi A4. Very impressed by the Bishop's vehicle, both Lexi and Carla gave compliments. "Yasss! Come on through, Bishop! This is nice," Carla said, clapping her hands. "Yasss, what she said!" Lexi chimed in. "Wow!" Bishop Goodwin said, shaking his head and laughing. "I can already tell you two are going to be so much fun to be around," First Lady Goodwin laughed as well. They all got into the car and went to the hometown fave Mrs. Helen's Place for lunch. Once they got there, the hostess took them to their table and gave them menus. Shortly after, a waiter came and took their orders. While waiting for their entrees, the four sparked a conversation to get to know everyone. Carla informed the Bishop and First Lady that she graduated with a degree in biology and eventually wants to go to med school. Bishop Goodwin shared that he was a lawyer before he went into ministry full time, and First Lady Goodwin is a family counselor. "So, Lexi, are you a student or working full time?" First Lady Goodwin asked. "Well, I am currently unemployed. I recently quit my job because it was a terrible place to work and I was so unhappy. I would love to get enrolled in school soon. I always wanted to do something in the field of social work or family counseling like you, First Lady," Lexi answered. "Valerie, do you still need an administrative assistant to help around the office?" Bishop Goodwin asked his wife. "As a matter of fact, I do! Do you have administrative experience?" First Lady Goodwin asked Lexi. "I don't. My work experience has pretty much been in retail and bar type environments," Lexi told First Lady beginning to feel a little embarrassed due to her lack of experience. "Well, Lexi, we serve a God who sometimes positions his people to get jobs they don't qualify for. This alignment is not coincidental. My lovely wife needs an administrative assistant and you need employment," the Bishop stated. "He's right! You may not have experience, but you are more than capable. I would be happy to have you and train you. This opportunity will also be great for you since you want to be a family counselor in the future," First Lady Goodwin happily told Lexi. "If this isn't God working! Val, tell her about the scholarship program that one of the saints mentioned a few weeks ago," Bishop said excitedly. "Oh, yeah, God is working! Thanks for bringing that up, dear. Well, one of the sisters at church works for the state. She's a social worker. Not too long ago, she announced that there is a program for students who are majoring in social work. Tuition will be fully paid in return for working for the state for two years after graduation. I will introduce you to her later this week. I mean, if this is something you are interested in," First Lady informed Lexi. Lexi, lost for words from all the information she just received, began to cry. "All I want to do is thank the Lord. I just want to scream 'Thank You, Jesus.' Thank you, Jesus!" Lexi said through joyful tears. "Yes, Lord. Won't he do it?" Carla said as her friend praised. "Thank you, Bishop and First Lady Goodwin! I am very interested in this program and working for you as well, First Lady," Lexi said before giving the First Lady a hug. They enjoyed their meals and conversed a little more, and then the Bishop and First Lady took Lexi and Carla back to Lexi's car at the church. When they returned to the church, First Lady told Lexi to come to her office in the morning to start her first day in her new position. They all said their goodbyes and the two cars went their separate ways.

A few days have passed and Lexi was adapting to her new role as an administrative assistant. First Lady Valerie has been very helpful and a great encouragement to Lexi. Lexi was finishing up some filing when First Lady came outside of her office with a family. "Lexi, can you schedule a follow-up appointment with the Sherrod's please?" "Of course!" "Thanks, Lexi" First Lady said as she waved good-bye to the Sherrod's and went back inside her office. "Okay, I have you all scheduled for next Friday at 2pm. Have a good evening," Lexi said cheerfully to the Sherrod's. Once the Sherrod's left, Lexi pulled out her cell phone that was vibrating as she was setting the appointment. It was a text message from Joc that read: "Thinking about you. Can't wait to see you later." Lexi grinned from ear to ear and texted him back that she was thinking about him as well and that she will see him soon. She put her phone away as First Lady Valerie came back out of her office. She walked over to Lexi's desk and handed her a folder. "Lexi, I've been meaning to give this to you. It's all the information you will need to enroll in the social work program at the community college. Tonight, I will introduce you to Sister Claudia. She will give you more insight on the program that will fully pay for your tuition." Lexi opened up the folder and went through some of the paperwork. "Thank you so much! I can't wait to begin the process," Lexi said, excitedly. "You're welcome! I know you will do great! And I will be with you every step of the way," First Lady Valerie said, and then leaned in to give Lexi a hug. Lexi felt comfort in First Lady's embrace. A feeling she hasn't felt in a long time. A motherly embrace. "I really appreciate all you are doing for me. I can't thank you enough," Lexi said as they ended their embrace. "I am happy to do it," First Lady began, and then turned her attention to the clock on the wall. "Well, the Sherrod's were my last appointment for today. So I am going to go get my things together and head on to the church. Are you looking forward to your first Youth Committee meeting?" "Yes. I am excited to see what's in store and how I can contribute," Lexi answered. First Lady smiled and nodded her head at Lexi's response, and then went into her office to gather her things. Lexi followed suit and shut down her computer to end her work day as well. She put on her sweater and grabbed her purse from underneath the desk. "Alrighty, let's get out of here," First Lady said, walking out of her office. Lexi followed her out the suite and stood with her as she locked the door. They said goodbye to the security guard on duty in the lobby and then exited the building. "Next time we leave the office to go straight to church, we should carpool," First Lady Valerie suggested. "I agree," Lexi nodded. "Sounds like a plan then. I will see you shortly, dear," First Lady said before the two ladies separated to their cars. Lexi got into her car and put on her seatbelt. Before starting the ignition, she took out her phone to see if Joc tried calling or texting her. She had a missed call from a private number and a couple of unread text messages. One of the text messages was from Carla reminding her of the youth meeting that evening. Lexi texted Carla back letting her know that she didn't forget. She opened the second unread message. It was from a number she didn't recognize. It was a picture message. Lexi had to tap on the picture in order for it to download. Lexi gasped and covered her mouth with one hand at the sight of the picture. She swallowed hard and began to breathe heavier at the sight of her naked image. "Who is this?" she texted the number. She immediately got another picture message from the anonymous person. It was another image of her, this time, naked straddling a man who was holding a large amount of cash. "What the—" she began before her phone buzzed with another text from the same number. She read the text aloud: "Secrets out! This is only the beginning."

Chapter 5

Lexi pulled into the church parking lot. She saw Carla and Joc waiting at the door for her. She got out of her car to join them. "Hey, Boo!" Carla greeted her with a hug. "Hey," Lexi said uneasy returning the hug. Lexi looked at Joc who was smiling at her presence. His smile is so contagious she couldn't help but smile back at him. They hugged briefly not wanting to cause too much attention to themselves. Joc held the door for the two ladies as they walked inside. "Follow me, ladies. We have the youth meetings downstairs," Joc said, leading the two. "Carla," Lexi whispered. Carla raised her eyebrows to signal Lexi that she has her attention. Lexi motioned for her to come closer to her. "Were you texting me as a joke earlier?" Lexi asked still whispering. "Huh? No. Why do you ask?" Carla whispered back. Lexi shook her head as to say never mind. "What are you two whispering about back there? Y'all better not be talking bad about me," Joc joked. "Yeah we are talkin' mad trash back here," Lexi joked back. "Don't do me like that. My feelings get hurt easily," Joc said, and then winked at Lexi. Lexi smiled, and then bit her bottom lip. "Like, eww. We are in church. I can't with you two," Carla said, acting disgusted. Lexi smiled and rolled her eyes at her friend. "Anyway, this is where the meeting is held," Joc said pointing to the room. He let the ladies enter first. It was about 20 other members in the room. The youth leader welcomed them as they came in and continued going over future events. The three sat together and listened as other members shared their ideas. Lexi felt as if someone was watching her. She looked across the table where she is sitting and made eye contact with Shalon. "Anyone else have any inputs?" the youth leader asked. Lexi raised her hand. The youth leader pointed to Lexi. "I was thinking maybe we can have a youth night every Friday. Sometimes we can do things here at the church like dinner and a movie. Possibly even have church in the park, or take the youth bowling and skating. This will allow the youth to fellowship with one another and possibly keep them from making poor choices over the weekend," Lexi shared. "I guess you could have used that growing up," Shalon mumbled. "Shalon, did you have an idea you wanted to share?" the youth leader asked noticing she had said something. Shalon shook her head no. "Lexi, I think that is a good idea. Does everyone else agree?" the youth leader asked. All of the members expressed that they wanted to schedule a youth night every Friday starting the next month. The meeting switched gears and the youth leader went on to talk about the mentoring program that Joc started for the male youth. As Joc went up to talk about the mentoring program, Bishop Goodwin and First Lady joined the meeting. "So as you all know, I started the mentoring program for the young fellas here. I lived a wild and crazy not-so-great lifestyle that ultimately almost caused me my life. So I just want to continue to share my experience with them so that they won't make the same mistakes that I made. I would like for more brothers to help being mentors. Also I think the young girls should have mentors from the sisters as well. We can be like a big brother and big sister program." "I would definitely like to help with the big sister program," Carla said. "I would, too." Lexi said, shaking her head in agreement. A few more female members volunteered to help as well. Shalon cleared her throat. "So what qualifications should one possess to be a mentor? We don't want our youth to be mentored by just anybody," Shalon said, briefly glancing at Lexi, and then directed her attention back to Joc for his answer. Lexi definitely felt shade coming from Shalon. "A mentor should be a good listener, motivator, share their experiences and knowledge, offer great advice and be a positive influence. Those are just a few qualities a mentor should have," Joc informed. "So would a prostitute or stripper be a positive influence for our young girls?" Shalon asked as she leaned back in her chair clasping her hands together in her lap. There was an awkward silence in the room. Joc hesitantly laughed. "Well, uhm. I mean that wouldn't be ideal. However, if that was a woman's past, I believe she could provide an insight on a path not to take," he answered. Lexi began to feel as if the room was closing in on her. *Is she referring to me?* Lexi thought. "Bishop, would you want a prostitute mentoring our young girls?" Shalon asked. Spencer the praise and worship leader was sitting next to Shalon. He bumped her arm with his elbow at her question. Shalon looked at Spencer and said, "Inquiring minds want to know." Bishop Goodwin scratched his head at the question. "Shalon, I agree with what Joc said." "Shalon, is there a reason why you keep asking the same question?" First Lady Goodwin asked. "I mean, I just want to know," Shalon answered. "Can we move on to another topic?" Carla interrupted. "Yes!" the youth leader said, taking back over the meeting. Lexi's phone vibrated. It was a text message from the same number that texted her earlier. The message was only a smiley face emoji. Lexi looked up from her phone and glanced at Shalon who was watching her. Shalon smiled at Lexi. *It's her!*

146

Lexi thought. *Why is she coming at me like this and how did she know about my past?* "OK, saints! Thanks for coming out tonight, next week we will we discuss some fundraising ideas to help fund the youth events to come," the youth leader said, bringing the meeting to an end. Everyone began to leave the room. "Lexi, bye, Angel-Eyes!" Shalon said aloud smiling and waving goodbye as Lexi was walking out the room. "Bye, Shalon, have a good night," Lexi said, playing it cool and keeping calm. "Don't work too hard tonight! How hard is it to slide down a pole, and then do a split?" Shalon smirked. Lexi was mortified. "That's enough! You stop right now!" Lexi warned getting in Shalon's face. "What's going on here?" Bishop Goodwin asked. Everyone was standing around confused at what was transpiring. "Why don't you ask that THOT!" Shalon yelled. Some of the members gasped in disbelief. "Why are you doing this to me? What did I do to you?" Lexi asked. "Cut it out, Shalon. What's up with you?" Joc asked. "Oh, I am sorry, Joc. I've been trying to figure out where I know your little girlfriend's face from. It turns out she's a stripper that accepts money for sex!" Shalon said sarcastically and maliciously. "I've had enough of this! Shalon go to my office, everyone else please leave," Bishop Goodwin instructed. "Not only is she a whore, she is a home wrecker! Everyone meet the slut my husband was screwing!" Shalon added more to the flame. Lexi glanced around at everyone staring at her, then she looked at Joc who was staring back at her puzzled. "I've been hurt many times in my life. But I would have never thought that I would be hurt in church." Lexi pushed through the members who were still standing around in shock. She walked as fast as she could to the nearest exit in the building. "Lexi! Lexi! Wait!" Carla called after her. Carla got in Shalon's face. "You picked the wrong one! I will lay hands on you. Hands!" Carla said, raising her fists. "Then I will pray for you like nothing ever happened. You don't want these problems, Ms. Hypocrite!" Carla threatened. "Yeah, I did a little research on you. Didn't you sleep with a married man for tuition money many years ago? And now you work for his company? Huh?" Carla spilled. "You're full of it!" Shalon bumped her chest against Carla's. "Ladies! Stop it! Just stop. This behavior is unacceptable at Kingdom Life Ministries. There is a time and place for everything and this was not the time or place to do so. You had no right to do that, Shalon," First Lady Valerie said, disappointed with Shalon's action. "Shalon, I am shocked at your actions. This is not like you. Please meet my wife and I in my office please," Bishop

Goodwin instructed. "Why is everyone staring at me like I am the bad guy? Lexi's the whore! And her ratchet sidekick just tried to fight me!" Shalon yelled. Carla shook her head in disgust at Shalon and pushed past her to go after Lexi. "My office now!" Bishop Goodwin said sternly and walked off with Lady Valerie.

Lexi ignored Carla calling after her, as she hurriedly got into her car and sped away. Lexi's mind was racing as she wished this was a horrible dream. She got to her apartment and entered inside. She shut her front door and slowly sat down on the floor with her back to the door. She cried at the humiliation she just experienced. All of a sudden, she was startled by a knock on her door. She figured it must be Carla coming to check up on her. She wiped her tears and stood up from the floor. Once she regained her composure, she opened the door. To her surprise, it was Joc. "Hey. Can I come in?" Joc asked. Lexi opened the door wider to let him inside. "Nice place," he complimented. "Thanks," she managed to say. "Have a seat. Would you like anything to drink?" she offered. "No, thanks. I'm good," he said, having a seat on her sofa. They sat in silence for a moment. Joc looked at the sliding door that led to Lexi's balcony. "You have a great view of the city. Can I step out to see the view?" "Sure," Lexi said, leading him to the balcony. "This is nice," he said, admiring the nighttime view of the city. "Yeah, I really like it," Lexi said, anticipating what Joc would say about what happened at the church. "Is any of it true?" he finally asked. "I am sorry, Joc," she said, ashamed. "So everything Shalon said is true?" "Yes, I used to be a stripper and I did do extra for money. But I am not like that anymore." "Why didn't you tell me?" "I didn't want to scare you away or for you to judge me before getting to know me." "Me, judge you? With my past, I could never judge you." "I am sorry for any embarrassment I may have caused you," Lexi said, tears beginning to roll down her face. "Baby girl, come here," Joc said, taking her by the hand and pulling her close to him. "No, I am sorry that you had to go through that," Lexi squeezed his hand with her head down not able to face him. "I understand if you don't want anything to do with me," she mumbled. Joc lifted Lexi's chin up and caressed her face. No words were exchanged. They just gazed into each other's eyes before engaging into a passionate kiss. The kiss was so intense that Joc picked Lexi up while still kissing her. Lexi wrapped her legs around Joc's waist as he carried her back inside her home. He sat on the sofa with Lexi still straddled on him. Caught up in the moment, Lexi began to take her clothes off while still kissing Joc. He gently bit her bottom lip then placed kisses all over her neck. Lexi stood up and leaned over Joc to unbuckle his belt. She then unzipped his pants and lowered herself to her knees to pleasure him. Realizing what was about to happen, Joc stopped Lexi before she could. "No. I can't let you do this," Joc said, trying to regain his composure. He straightened himself up and helped Lexi to her feet. "What? Why?" she asked confused. "I don't want you—" he began before Lexi interrupted. "I understand," she said, putting her clothes back on. "I get it. I've been around and you don't want me in this way. What was I thinking?" "No, you don't understand. I do want you in this way, but not this way. Not like this, not now," he explained. "Trust me, if you met me before I got saved we would both have carpet burns right now!" he said, causing Lexi to shake her head and smile. "I want to get to know Alexis. I don't just wanna see you naked and touch your body. I want to know what makes you happy, what makes you cry, and laugh. I want to know your dreams and aspirations. I see your cover now I want to open you up and read you." Lost for words and filled with emotions, Lexi hugged Joc. He held her back and kissed the top of her head. "Lexi?" "Yes, Joc? "Just know you can tell me anything and I won't ever make you feel ashamed. Okay?" Lexi shook her head yes and rest her head on his shoulder.

The next day, Lexi agreed to meet up with First Lady Valerie at the church. At first, Lexi wasn't going to come. She even thought about leaving the church altogether. All she could think about were all the faces that stared at her in shock after she was humiliated. But after praying and a heart to heart with First Lady, here she stands. It was a Saturday, so not too much activity was going on there. Lexi walked into the church and entered the sanctuary. No one was inside, so she took a seat on a pew in the front row. She began to reflect on how drastically her life has changed within a couple of weeks. Real employment she wasn't ashamed of, a new church home, a special friend, and a fresh start. Lexi's thoughts were interrupted by footsteps. She turned around to see Bishop and First Lady approaching her. "Hi, Lexi! How are you?" First Lady greeted her with a hug. "I am fine. Thanks for asking. How are you?" Lexi said after their embrace. "I am well. We've been thinking about you all night," First Lady said. "Yes, Lexi, you have been on our minds and in our prayers. Please don't let what happened last night be a reflection of us or the church as a whole. We don't care what you did in your past, we love you the same," Bishop Goodwin assured her. "Thanks. Of all places, I never thought that I would be publicly humiliated in the church. But in spite of it all, I am okay. I am no longer going to let my past control or make me feel less than or ashamed," Lexi said, finally feeling free. "That's right, honey! You keep your head up just like that," First Lady encouraged her. "Lexi, when I was praying for you last night, God told me to take you in as a daughter. So I am going to obey him. We promise that we will always be here for you and cover you as if you were our flesh and blood," Bishop Goodwin said with a sincere heart. Lexi looked at them both taken back by what Bishop said. "Really?" Lexi beginning to tear up. Bishop Goodwin and First Lady Valerie glanced at each other, and then at Lexi and both smiled and shook their heads yes. "I am almost lost for words. All I ever wanted was a mother's love. But to be blessed with a mother and a father after all these years, I am so thankful." Lexi stood up to embrace them. As they embraced her back, Lexi began to pray: "Lord I thank You for Your grace and mercy. Thank You for catching all my tears and never turning Your back on me. Thank You for saving me from myself. Thank You for getting me to a place of surrender. I now know that I had to be broken down so low that I had no choice but to look up and call on You. I am not where I want to be, but I am far from who I use to be. And I know with You as my guide and these two by my side I will be the woman that You created me to be. I love You so much! Amen."

Forced Out

Chapter 1

"Thanks for picking up an extra shift tonight," Reese's manager thanked him. "No problem! I needed the extra hours anyway," Reese told his manager. Reese went to the employee break room to grab his things out of his locker. Reese has been working part time at Mrs. Helen's Place as a waiter for a couple months now to help pay his way through school. He is a sophomore in college studying Theater. He is an aspiring actor and hopes to make a name for himself in Hollywood one day. Reese is well put together. He has always been voted best dressed from grade school to now. He is an average height for a man and decent weight. He has a paper bag brown complexion with a short curly haircut. Reese grabbed his bag to fish for his cell phone that is vibrating. Once he retrieved it, he noticed he has 4 missed calls and 6 unread text messages. *Wow, who is blowing my phone up like this?* he thought to himself. He saw he had two missed calls from his best friend, one from his mother, and one from someone he has recently started dating. He opened up his missed text messages and read them all and responded to let the other parties know that he just got off work. Reese gathered the rest of his belonging and headed out the break room so he could clock out. After he clocked out, he said his goodbyes to his co-workers who were still working. "Hey, Mom!" he said into his phone as he walked to his car. "Hey, baby! I didn't know you had to work today," his mom told him. "Yeah, we are so short staffed right now that I couldn't say no to helping out. Plus, I needed the extra money," he let his mom know. "Well, sweetie, I was just checking on you. You know I miss you so much when you are away at school," his mom shared. "Awww. I know, Mom. I miss you, too! I'll be home for spring break soon," Reese said. Reese and his mother are very close. And being that Reese is an only child, he is somewhat of a Mama's boy. They talked for a little while longer until an incoming call came in on the other line. It was his new boo, Tracy, calling. "Well, Mom, you know I love talking to you for hours, but I got to go," he told her. His mother sucked her teeth and said, "Mmm-hmm. I know it's your new boo-thang clicking in!" They both laughed and said their goodbyes. Reese accepted the incoming call. "Hey, you!" he said in a very soft voice. "Hey, to you!" Tracy said back. "How was your day?" Reese asked. "Even better now that I am talking to you," Tracy replied. "Can I see you tonight?" Tracy asked. "I would love to see you, but I have a ton of homework to do," Reese said, starting to feel bummed from declining the invitation. "Maybe I can help you with your homework," Tracy offered. With a smile, Reese said, "You are so sweet!" "Sweet on you," Tracy said flirtatiously. Reese was exiting off the interstate when his car started shaking and smoke began coming from under the hood. "Not again!" Reese said frustrated as he pulled over to the side of the road. "Is everything okay?" Tracy asked concerned. "No, it's my car. It's been acting up for a while now," Reese answered. "Do you need me to come help you?" Tracy offered. "Yes, please, I would really appreciate it," Reese replied. Reese informed his love interest of his location. Reese got out of his car and lifted the hood. The smoke cleared away but being that Reese didn't know anything about cars, he decided to not touch anything. He went back into his car and tried to start it up and once again, the car began to shake. *Doesn't look like I will be driving anywhere else tonight,* he thought to himself. He took his key out of the ignition, and then searched for his AAA card in his wallet. He called AAA to let them know he is in need of roadside assistance. The dispatcher he spoke with informed him that a tow truck was on the way. Reese saw that a car pulled up behind him with its lights flashing as he ended his phone call. It was Tracy. Reese and Tracy both got out of their cars. "Thank you so much for coming!" Reese said as he hugged Tracy. "No problem! I am always here if you need me," Tracy assured Reese. "What's been going on with your car?" Tracy asked. "For about a month now it has been shaking every now and then, but tonight is the first time I've seen it smoke," Reese informed Tracy. "I called AAA and they are on the way to tow it." "Where are you having it towed?" Tracy asked. "To my place, I don't know any mechanics here," Reese answered. "You can have your car towed to my mechanic. He is awesome and he reasonably prices his services. I will call him now to let him know your car will be towed there," Tracy said. Tracy stepped away to make the phone call to his mechanic. A few minutes later, Tracy returned. "Everything is set, my mechanic will look at your car first thing in the morning," Tracy informed Reese. "Thank you so much, you are the best!" Reese said as he hugged Tracy. The tow truck finally came. Reese gave the tow truck driver the address to Tracy's mechanic's shop. Tracy gave Reese a ride home. Once they got to Reese's apartment, they both got out of the car and walked to Reese's doorstep. "Well, it looks like I got to see you tonight after all," Tracy said with a smile. "Funny how things work out," Reese said before giving Tracy a kiss on the cheek. "And now that you are here, why don't you come in and help me with my homework?" Reese said, biting his bottom lip. Tracy entered the apartment before Reese and said, "Invitation accepted."

***

Brinng! Brinng! Tracy's telephone rang loudly. Waking Reese up. "Baby! Wake up, your phone is ringing." Reese gently shook Tracy's shoulder. Tracy woke up and answered the phone. "Hello. This is Tracy," Reese watched Tracy sit up in the bed. The sunlight is peeking inside the curtains and shining on Tracy's back. *Mmmm that body is everything!* Reese thought to himself admiring Tracy's well-defined v-shaped back and muscular arms. Tracy got up and paced the room back and forth as he talked on the phone. This gave Reese and even better view of his body. Tracy is in his early 40's, average height, has a muscular build, a bald head, a well-groomed beard, and very dark complexion. Reese met him at his job—Mrs. Helen's Place —and they hit it off right away. "Finally! I thought that call would never end," Reese said playfully as Tracy got back in the bed. "Work related, I am always on call. But you got my attention now. How did you sleep?" Tracy said as he lay down next to Reese "I slept well. Especially being in your arms all night," Reese replied. "It felt nice holding you," Tracy said, rubbing Reese's arm. Reese's phone began to ring. "Hello… This is him… Wow, it's that bad? How much will it cost to repair? Oh. Okay. Let me make a few phone calls and I will call you back. OK. Thank you." Reese ended the call. "Was that my mechanic?" Tracy asked "Yes." "What did he say?" "It's my engine. He said my engine is pretty much toast and I need a new one. He estimates it may cost me $2500 to be repaired. I don't have that kind of money. I can barely afford tuition and all my living expenses. Now this!" Reese said, feeling stressed. "Don't worry, I'll take care of it for you." Tracy reached on the nightstand and grabbed his phone. "Give me your bank account information. I will wire you the funds. Then call my mechanic back and tell him to start working on it," Tracy said. "Are you serious? Please don't play with me like this! For real for real?" Reese said, surprised. "Yes! I am serious. Now give me your bank info." "Omg! Thank you so much," Reese said, giving Tracy a big hug. "I really appreciate your generosity, but it may take me awhile to pay you back." "It's okay. Consider it a gift," Tracy told him. "Wow! You are awesome. Even though you said it's a gift, I owe you big! You are a godsend!" Reese said, planting a kiss on Tracy before going to his desk to get his bank information. "Just do me a favor," Tracy began. "Anything!" Reese quickly said. "If my mechanic asks how you know me, tell him I am your mentor. Okay?" Tracy said, walking up to Reese's desk. "My mentor? Why?" Reese asked confused. "No one can know about us. No one," Tracy said in a calm but serious tone. "Are you ashamed of me? Are you married? Let me guess you're on the down low." Reese bombarded Tracy with questions. "Listen, I like you a lot and love being around you. But I have a lot on the line here. No one can know." Tracy kissed Reese on the forehead, and then began to get dressed. Reese decided to leave well enough alone. At least for now. Reese called the mechanic back and told him to start the labor right away. He was told that his car will be ready for pick up in a couple of days. Reese relayed the news to Tracy. Tracy took Reese to a car rental establishment and rented him a car. "Thank you so much, babe, for everything," Reese said as he got into the rental car. "You're welcome! Call me when you get out of class," Tracy said as he shut the door for Reese. Reese blew Tracy a kiss and Tracy smiled and winked at the gesture. The two went their separate ways. On Reese's drive to class, he received a call from his best friend, Thea.

"Hey, Reesee Poo!" Thea's voice blared through the phone. "Hey, The-The baby!" he said, happy to hear from his friend. "So like, you been M-I-A for days. What's the tea bish?" Thea asked of her friend's whereabouts. Reese thought about the last few days he has spent with Tracy. He smiled at the thought. "Girl, you know school and work keep me busy," he said, knowing his friend would not go for that answer. "School and work have never kept you from ripping and running with me. So who is he?" Thea asked still waiting on the details. "Okay girl! Since you must know. I have a little friend. We have been hanging out or what not. I am really feeling him, but, honey, we will see how it goes," Reese informed his friend. "Well, you're going to have to tell me more about him. Let's meet up for lunch today. I need to see my bestie!" Thea said. "Okay, boo, I will call you after class," Reese said as he pulled up to his school. The two said their goodbyes.

Reese could barely keep his eyes open during his Professor's history lecture. *Omigod this is so boring*, Reese thought to himself. He doodled on his notepad to try to stay awake. Thoughts of Tracy came to his mind. Reese is really feeling Tracy and he loves his generosity. But the whole 'nobody must know about us' spill that Tracy gave this morning is a big red flag for Reese. Reese continued in thought. *I guess I got to do some research on him. Lord, please don't let him be married.* Reese pulled out his phone and did a reverse phone look up on Tracy's phone number. He was able to find Tracy's full name, address, and possible relatives. Just with this little piece of information, Reese has already found out that Tracy has lied about his last name. Tracy told Reese that his last name is Lee. However, according to this search, it's West. *Tracy West, huh? I wonder what else he's not being honest about,* Reese thought to himself. Reese didn't want to overreact, but two red flags have presented themselves within a few hours. And one thing Reese doesn't put up with is being lied to or being a side piece. After his previous drama-filled relationship, he made a vow that the next man that came to him with that "let's keep us a secret" crap he would expose. When class was dismissed, Reese grabbed his things to leave; he looked at his screen saver, a picture of Tracy on his phone. "Tracy baby, I hope you are who you say you are. Because I would hate to expose you," Reese said to himself and headed to his next class.

Chapter 2

Reese met up with Thea for lunch. She got there before him, so she was already sitting at their table. Reese spotted her and made his way over. "That's my best friend, that's my best friend, yasss!" Thea greeted Reese in a sing-song manner. She stood up and gave him a big hug. "Yasss, darlin', yasss! You are super snatched." Reese grabbed Thea by the hand to spin her around. "You are working this dress! Team curves, team slim thick, team no waist—" "And let's not forget team cute face!" Thea interrupted flipping her hair, smiling with her tongue between her teeth. Reese frowned. "See, I was trying to be nice and give a couple compliments, but you just had to be extra. You know darn well you don't have a cute face!" Reese said and sat down. "You play too much." Thea rolled her eyes. "Nah, honey, you're ugly. Now sit down." "Awww, you missed me! That's the only time you talk crazy to me," Thea said as she sat down. "Girl, you know I did. I had to throw a few shots to make up for lost time, but you know I love you," Reese replied squeezing Thea's hand. The two continued to tease each other and catch up with one another. Reese gave all the deets on Tracy to bring Thea up to speed. Reese noticed someone has caught Thea's attention. She was watching a gentleman's every move with lust in her eyes as she bit her index finger. "Ooh, he is too fine," she managed to say. Reese looked in the direction she was staring. He immediately put the menu to the side of his face so he couldn't be seen. "Omigod! That's Tracy," Reese said through his teeth. "That's Tracy? Wow!" Thea spoke still looking at Tracy. "Yes! So stop looking at him like a dog in heat, you lil' thirsty trick," Reese scolded. "Whoa! My bad, sorry. Anyway, why are you hiding?" Thea asked. "Remember, I just told you I feel like he is hiding something. I don't want him to see me, this gives me a chance to see if he's meeting up with perhaps a wife or girlfriend," Reese responded. "Okay, well you should at least put the menu down. That's just going to cause attention to yourself. I'm just saying," Thea suggested. Reese rolled his eyes at Thea even though he knew she was right. A few minutes had gone by and Tracy was still sitting alone at his table. Reese watched Tracy place his order and hand his menu to the waitress. "It doesn't look like he's meeting anyone here, I would think he would wait to order if he was," Thea observed. "I think you're right, but I still want to be sure," Reese said, pulling out his phone. "I am about to text him." "Thinking about you! ☺" Reese texted. A few seconds later, Tracy responded. "Thinking of you, too!" "Are you working hard or hardly working?" Reese texted back. "Hardly working, I am on a lunch break. You can call me if you are free right now," Tracy replied. Reese looked up from his phone and over at Tracy who was now eating. "So what did he say?" Thea asked. "That he's at lunch and I can call him. Should I?" "Yes! Call him now," Thea said, picking up Reese's phone and pressing the phone receiver icon by Tracy's name. Reese's eyes got big once he noticed that the call had already been placed. "I'm gonna get you!" Reese whispered to his friend. "Hey, You!" Reese said softly once he heard Tracy's voice. "Hey, what are you up to?" Tracy asked "Oh, just having lunch with my friend, telling her all about you," Reese responded. "Oh, really? I hope you told her I am the perfect guy," Tracy said. "I did. I can't wait to see you later, maybe we can meet up before you go back to work," Reese said to see what Tracy's response would be. "Sure, where are you? I can meet you somewhere nearby," Was Tracy's reply. "I am at this little Mexican restaurant near downtown. It's called Casa de Tacos," Reese informed. There was a brief silence on Tracy's end. Reese watched Tracy glance around the restaurant. Reese lifted his menu to cover his face. "I just remembered I have a meeting back at the office in about 15 minutes. We can meet up later. I'll talk to you soon," Tracy said and hung up before Reese could respond. Reese watched Tracy leave some cash on his table and immediately leave the establishment. "OK, so I am convinced he's hiding something," Reese said getting upset. "Calm down, I am going to see what I can find out," Thea said and motioned for the waitress who was waiting on Tracy to come over. "Hola! How can I help you?" the waitress asked. "Hi! There was a guy sitting at that table you were serving. Does he come here a lot?" Thea asked "Actually, he does; he works nearby, so he's always a part of the lunch crowd," the waitress informed. "He's pretty hot! Do you know if he's single?" Thea asked. "I am not really sure, he usually comes alone or with coworkers," The waitress answered. "OK, thank you so much. I hope I run into him again," Thea smiled. "You're welcome! I am pretty sure you will. Like I said, he's a regular part of our lunch crowd. Let me know if you two need anything," the waitress said and left their table. "He's definitely on the down low. He left because he didn't want anyone to see him with me," Reese said as the two got up to leave. "Just chill out. I don't want you to over-react without all the facts," Thea advised. Reese walked Thea to her car and they promised they would talk later that night. Reese went back to his rental car. As he was putting on his seat belt, his attention was drawn to the commercial building across the street. The swanky building housed several businesses. One particular business stood out to Reese. West and Lane Management. Reese made note of the address so he could further investigate later. He pulled away from the restaurant and headed home.

A few hours had passed. Reese came home and did a little studying, cleaned his apartment, and was now laying on his sofa channel surfing. "All these channels and nothing is on," Reese said to himself. Reese's phone rang. He didn't recognize the number but decided to answer anyway. "Hello, this is Reese." "Hi, Reese, my name is Alvin. I am the mechanic that worked on your car." "Oh, hi! Please give me some good news," Reese said. "Well I do have some good news for you. Your car is ready for pick up. I finished the repairs earlier than expected. You can come now if you want," Alvin informed. "Okay, great! I am currently using a rental car so I will need to call someone to bring me to your shop," Reese told Alvin. "Sounds like a plan, I'll see you soon," Alvin responded. Reese ended the call and was about to call Tracy to tell him the news, but decided not to. Instead, he called Thea. Thea came and got Reese and took him to Alvin's shop. "Thank you, boo! You are the best," Reese said as he gave Thea a hug and got out the car. "You're Welcome! I am going to stay right here until you get your car," Thea said. "Okay, thanks, hon," Reese said, and then walked into the shop. Reese looked around the lobby to speak with someone. There was a bell on what looks like a receptionist desk, so Reese tapped it. "Hello, is anybody here?" Reese called out. A few seconds later, a man walked out from the back. "Hello, how may I help you?" the man asked. "I am here to pick up my car," Reese answered. The man stood behind the receptionist desk to log into his computer. "What is your name and the make and model of your vehicle?" "Reese Carothers, Ford Taurus," Reese replied. "Oh, Reese. I just spoke with you on the phone. I am Alvin," Alvin informed. Alvin printed off Reese's receipt and handed him his keys. "Your car is ready out front." "Thank you so much!" Reese said happily. "Before you leave, I almost forgot to ask. Did someone refer you? I like to send out a token of appreciation to my customers who spread the word about me." "Uhm, yes. A guy named Tracy suggested you," Reese hesitated to say. "Oh, yeah? Tracy West! He's a good friend of mine, I consider him my brother. How do you know him?" Alvin inquired. Reese didn't respond right away.

He thought about what Tracy told him earlier if he was asked this question. "He's one of my mentors, he was recommended by one of my professors at the university I attend," Reese lied. "Are you majoring in business? He has a successful business management firm, you will learn a lot from him," Alvin waited on Reese to answer. Reese cleared his throat. "Yes, I am business major. He is definitely a plethora of knowledge," Reese lied again. "Well it was nice meeting you, Reese. God bless you and have a good night." "Thank you and you have a good night as well," Reese said, and then left the shop. He located his car and got in. Before pulling off, he waved at Thea to signal that she could leave now. Reese looked at the time on his dashboard. It was 6:00. He figured Tracy should be off work by now and decided to call him. Tracy answered. "Hey, I will call you right back," Tracy said quickly, and then hung up. "What the fu—" Before Reese could finish his sentence, his phone rang. It was Tracy. "Hello!" Reese answered slightly annoyed. "Sorry about that, I was on the other line with a vendor," Tracy apologized. "Oh, okay. I just left your mechanic. My car is running great," Reese informed Tracy. "Awesome, he's the best at what he does," Tracy said. "I believe you, I don't think my car has ever driven this smooth."

"So did you tell him anything?" Tracy questioned "What do mean?" Reese asked. "You know… about us" Tracy answered, "No. He asked how do I know you and I told him you are my mentor." "Good," Tracy said, relieved. Reese rolled his eyes but kept calm. "So will I see you tonight?" "Yes, it will be late, though. Maybe after 10," Tracy told him. "Why so late?" Reese wanted to know. "I go to church on Wednesdays. Bible study," Tracy informed. "Oh, I see. Well I guess I'll see you later tonight," Reese said, wrapping up the conversation. "Sounds like a plan," Tracy confirmed. The two ended their conversation. Once Reese got home, he decided to do some digging on Tracy. He pulled out all the information he gathered from the day. He found out that Tracy has owned his home for five years, and has been a business owner for ten years—which didn't seem out of the ordinary. Reese logged into his Facebook account to see if he could find Tracy on there. He typed in Tracy West in the search engine and many profiles returned. Reese narrowed his search and couldn't find a profile for Tracy. Reese then searched for the possible relatives of Tracy that he found during the reverse phone look up earlier. Still, no hits. Reese even searched Facebook to see if Tracy had a business page for his company. *I give up*, Reese thought after not finding anything on Facebook. Just as he was about to log off, he remembered the mechanic, Alvin. He grabbed the receipt from his car repairs to get Alvin's full name off it. *He probably doesn't even have an account being that he's an older man. Who am I kidding? Almost everyone has a Facebook account,* Reese thought. "Alvin Roberts," Reese said as he typed in the search engine. "Bingo!" Reese said when he found Alvin's profile. Alvin's page didn't have much activity on it or photos. Reese did come across a photo of Alvin with a young woman. Must be his daughter, Reese thought. Alvin was tagged in the photo by a church. Reese clicked on the name of the church to view its page. Kingdom Life Ministries. Reese skimmed through the pictures and came across several with Tracy in them. Most of the photos Tracy was in he was with his pastor. I wonder what his role is at this church, Reese thought. "Well, at least I know for sure now he's not married," Reese said as he closed his laptop. Reese was doing so much Facebook lurking that he lost track of time. "It is 10:30!" He jumped up to go take a shower anticipating Tracy's visit. Not too long after, Reese could hear Tracy calling for him. "Reese...Reese, I am here." Tracy wandered around Reese's apartment searching for him. Reese purposely left his front door unlocked for him to come in. "I am in the shower, babe!" Reese yelled. Reese grabbed a towel to wrap around his waist. He stepped out the shower and opened his bathroom door to Tracy standing there. "Well, hello!" Tracy said, biting his bottom lip. Reese was about to say hello back but before he could, Tracy put his index finger in front of his lips indicating for Reese to keep silent. Tracy grabbed Reese by his face and gave him a steamy kiss. Reese removed Tracy's jacket and loosened his tie. Tracy unbuttoned his shirt while Reese unzipped his pants. "I want you so bad!" Reese whispered loudly and aggressively pushed Tracy to the wall. Reese bit Tracy's bottom lip, and then hungrily kissed him. Tracy returned the kiss wanting Reese just as bad. Tracy pulled away from the kiss and ordered Reese to turn around. Reese obeyed. Tracy wrapped one arm around Reese's waist to pull him closer to him. With his free hand he grabbed Reese by his throat. Reese laid his head back on Tracy's shoulder with his mouth open breathing hard. "How bad to you want me?" Tracy asked applying more pressure to Reese's throat. "Really bad!" Reese answered. "You sure this is what you want? Tracy asked letting go of Reese's neck. Reese turned around to face Tracy and shook his head yes. "Well, lead the way," Tracy instructed, and then followed Reese to his bedroom.

Reese woke up to Tracy tapping on his shoulder. "Good morning," Reese said through his yawn. "Good morning," Tracy reciprocated. "What time is it?" Reese asked sitting up in bed to look at his alarm clock. "Still, pretty early," Tracy replied. "You're not lying, it's 5am. This is entirely too early for me," Reese said, lying back down and pulling his covers under his chin. Tracy got out of the bed and began to put his clothes on. "What are you doing?" Reese asked now sitting back up in his bed. Tracy was silent, he continued to get dress. "Are you leaving?" Reese asked confused. Tracy stopped what he was doing to finally answer Reese. "Yes. I have to go." "But why so early?" Reese got out of bed and stood in front of Tracy. Tracy stepped back so that there was space between the two. He rubbed his hands together, and then took a deep breath and exhaled. "Look...I can't do this anymore," Tracy said, and then sat on the edge of Reese's bed to put his shoes on. "You can't do what anymore?" "This thing we have going on. I don't want to do it anymore," Tracy said. "Soooo, what has brought this on?" Reese said, getting agitated. "I don't have to explain my reasons," Tracy said in a cold tone as he got up to leave the bedroom. Tracy's tone took Reese off guard. Reese ran to his bedroom door and stood in front of it so Tracy couldn't exit.

"Yes, you do have to explain! What is this about? I mean, you were just all over me!" "Reese, it's over. I don't want to see you again. Now get out of my way so that I can leave." Reese shook his head in disbelief. "No, sir; no, ma'am! I am not moving. You can at least be man enough to tell me why you've suddenly had a change of heart." Tracy began to crack his knuckles. "I am sorry. You're right, I do owe you an explanation. So here it is… I am not interested in being in a relationship with you or any man for that matter. I am not gay. Sorry, I led you on. I am willing to pay you generously to move on as if we never met," Tracy said, pulling out an envelope of cash out of his jacket pocket. Reese grabbed the envelope and threw it on the floor. "You're not gay? What? You're not gay?" Reese said loudly and sarcastically. Reese laughed loudly at the foolery he just heard. "Oh, baby boo, I hate to tell you this but YOU'RE GAY, honey!" Reese continued to block the doorway. "Either we can do this the easy way or we can do this the hard way. Easy way, you move on your own. Hard way, I will move you. And I promise you don't want that," Tracy said calmly. Reese, unfazed by Tracy's threat, crossed his arms across his chest and didn't move. "I am so sick and tired of you down low brothas that convince yourselves that you are not gay. If you get turned on by another man, you're gay! If you receive any sexual favors from another man, you're gay! If you have sex with another man… Say it with me… YOU'RE GAY," Tired of hearing Reese's mouth, Tracy grabbed Reese by the throat and pushed him out of the bedroom door into the hallway wall. "You like being choked, huh? Just a little more pressure and you will be dead. I told you it's over! Respect it." Tracy let go of Reese and watched him collapse to the ground. Reese rubbed his neck trying to catch his breath. Reese looked up at Tracy who was now headed to the front door. Tracy stopped before leaving out. "Oh yeah, you can have that money in the envelope. Remember, we never met." Reese, still out of breath, watched Tracy leave. "You think this is over? You think this is a game? Play with me if you want to. You picked the wrong one," Reese said vengefully.

Chapter 3

A couple of weeks have gone by since Tracy broke things off with Reese. Tracy changed his phone number thinking that would cut off all ties with Reese. But what Tracy doesn't know is Reese knows more about him than he thinks. Reese has been following Tracy. Reese knows Monday through Friday Tracy leaves his home every morning at 8:30 and gets to his office at 9am. He leaves his office at 5:30pm and makes it home around 6:15 every evening except on the nights he goes to church, which is on Wednesdays and Fridays. On those nights, he gets home around 9. Reese even knows Tracy's weekend schedule, which is mostly spent at his church. Thanks to social media, Reese found out that Tracy is his pastor's armor bearer and has recently started dating a woman named Claudia. And thanks to Thea who works at the bank Tracy banks with, Reese now knows that Tracy is sitting on a lot of money. Still bitter from the abrupt breakup and tired of dealing with down low men, Reese has plotted to expose Tracy.

"Hi! Welcome to West and Lane Management. How may I help you?" the receptionist at the front desk greeted Reese. "Hello, I am looking for Tracy West. I have a meeting scheduled," Reese replied. The receptionist looked at her computer, and then at her appointment sheet on her desk. Tracy didn't have any meeting scheduled today. "I am sorry, I can't find your appointment. What time is your meeting?" the receptionist asked still searching. Reese looked up at the clock behind the receptionist. The time read 10:00. "It's at 10," Reese said with a smile. "I set all the appointments, I can't believe I forgot to put it in," the receptionist said of the error. "Oh no, I actually made the appointment with Mr. West," Reese told her. "Oh! Okay. Whew! I am still kind of new, I can't afford to make any mistakes," the receptionist said, relieved. "What is your name so I can tell him you are here?" the receptionist asked. "Reese Carothers." The receptionist called Tracy: "Hi, Mr. West. Your 10:00 appointment is here..... His name is Reese Carothers...Uhm, I didn't set the appointment. He said he made it with you...Okay, sir." The receptionist put the call with Tracy on mute and looked up at Reese. "Mr. West doesn't remember setting an appointment with you. What is the meeting about?" "That's kind of unprofessional," Reese said, putting his hands in front of him to look at his manicured nails. "I am sorry," the receptionist said nervously. "Tell him I am a student from Merriam's University. He was assigned to me as a mentor." The receptionist relayed the message to Tracy. A few minutes later, Tracy came out his office. Tracy had a stern demeanor and he was clearly annoyed by Reese's presence. "Well, hello, Mr. West!" Reese said with a big smile on his face. Tracy nodded his head and forced a smile. Tracy signaled Reese to follow him to his office. "Ooh, this is nice!" Reese said, admiring Tracy's workspace. "I don't have time for this. This is my place of business. I've never told you where I work. So how did you find me and what brings you here?" Tracy said, shutting his office door. "First of all, we live in a world where privacy doesn't exist anymore. And secondly, I came to see you, boo! I need you to mentor me," Reese said, sitting in Tracy's executive style office chair. Tracy walked over to his chair to pull Reese out of it. "I am not mentoring you and get your raggedy ass out of my seat." "Excuse you! You're so rude," Reese said as he got up from Tracy's chair and moved to the chair in front of Tracy's desk. "If my memory serves me right, I thought I said I didn't want to see you again. Do I need to give you another reminder?" Tracy said and began to crack his knuckles. Reese raised his hands as if he was surrendering. "Relax. You won't have to choke-a-hoe today." Reese shook his head and rolled his eyes. "And I don't need a mentor...I need a sponsor,"

Reese smirked. "Okay, I see what this is about. You want more money. How much?" Tracy reached into his desk drawer and pulled out his checkbook. "$20000 cash and no one will ever know about us," Reese said without hesitation. Tracy frowned at the number "$20000? You have lost your damn mind! I am not giving you $20000." "Well I guess I'm going to spill the beans about your nasty little deeds," Reese sneered. Tracy closed his eyes and took a deep breath and exhaled. He got up from his seat and exited his office. He returned with a briefcase. Tracy placed the briefcase on his desk and opened it. Several bank deposit bags fell out. Reese watched as Tracy counted out $20000. "Happy now?" Tracy asked slamming the wad of money in front of Reese. Reese grabbed the money and flipped through the bills smiling from ear to ear. "Yes, sir, I am." "OK, good. You can leave now!" Tracy dismissed. Reese got up to leave and Tracy grabbed his arm. "Don't ever come here again and don't open your mouth to anyone," Tracy said through clenched teeth. Reese pulled away from Tracy's grasp. "Don't worry, your secret is safe with me." Reese exited Tracy's office and closed the door behind him. "Your secret is safe for now," Reese said to himself and left the building.

"Hey, Reese, you are needed up front. The after-church crowd is here." Reese's manager informed him. "Okay, I'll be right out," Reese said, picking up his pen and pad. "I can't even take a full 15 minute break without being bothered," Reese mumbled under his breath as he made his way up front. Reese doesn't like working on Sundays. It's always extremely busy, which is great for business, that one would think it would be great for the waiters and waitresses as well. But that's not the case on Sundays. *These church folks come in, by the dozen, judge you, push their beliefs on you, eat up everything and tip poorly. Woosah!* Reese thought to himself as he looked at the table of 8 he was assigned to. Reese made his way over to the guest and introduced himself. "Hello, my name is Reese. I will be you all's waiter today." Reese handed the guests menus and began to take their drink orders. One of the women sitting at the table looked familiar to Reese. He studied her face for a moment and realized he remembered her picture from Facebook on the mechanic's profile. "Are you all just getting out of church?" Reese asked. The group informed him that they did just get out of church and told him how awesome service was. One lady even gave Reese a card with the church info on it. "You should come visit us," she invited. "We would love to have you," the woman he recognized from Facebook chimed in. "I am Tara by the way," she introduced herself. "Nice to meet you, I will definitely come on one of my free Sundays," Reese said and put the card in his pocket. "I will be back with your drinks soon," he said and left the table. As he was leaving, he overheard a couple of women at the table whispering: "Why would you invite that sissy to our church?" "Well, clearly, he's needs to be there to get rid of those demons he's carrying." "Yes, he needs to be delivert!" Two of the women laughed. "You two are so mean spirited. Clearly, that is something you both need to be delivered from," Tara said disappointed by their behavior. Reese let the comments roll off his back. He has heard them so much that it doesn't even bother him anymore. However, he does find it odd that the same people who are taught to love everyone attacks him the most. "That's church folk for ya," Reese said to himself. Reese served the ladies their drinks and took their meal orders. After putting the orders into the kitchen staff, he went to his next table. To his surprise, Tracy was at the table with four others: Claudia, his new lady, his pastor and his wife, and Alvin, the mechanic who Reese found out is a deacon. Tracy avoided eye contact with Reese and didn't acknowledge him, although the rest of the table did. "You all have on your

Sunday best, I know y'all had some good church today!" Reese said to the table. "And you two look so good, I would assume you are a pastor and you're his first lady," Reese continued to warm chat directing his comment to Tracy's pastor. "You assumed right. I am Bishop Eugene Goodwin. I pastor at Kingdom Life Ministries and this is my beautiful wife, Valerie," Bishop Goodwin said proudly. "Hey, do you remember me? I am Alvin. I worked on your car not too long ago. How have you been?" "Yes, I do remember you. I am great! Thanks for asking," Reese responded. Reese could tell that Tracy was getting uncomfortable. "Thanks, Tracy man, for referring him to my shop, brotha," Alvin thanked Tracy. "No problem, anything to support your business," Tracy said and cleared his throat. "How do you two know each other?" Lady Valerie asked. "I've been mentoring a few of the students over at Merriam. I helped Reese with a project a little while ago," Tracy lied. "I am a M.U. alumna. How do you like it there?" Claudia asked. "I love it!" Reese told her. The longer Reese stood there, more and more sweat beads formed on Tracy's head. Reese wanted to laugh but kept his composure. *Aww, po' tink-tink, I am really about to make you squirm now,* Reese thought to himself. "Kingdom Life Ministries. I have heard so many good things about your church lately. I would love to come visit sometime." Tracy stared at Reese coldly after he made the statement. No one noticed but Reese. "Yes! You should definitely come visit us," Bishop Goodwin said enthusiastically. The rest of the table besides Tracy agreed. Tracy cleared his throat once more and loosened his tie. "It's kind of hot in here. Can I get some water please?" Tracy hinted for Reese to leave. "Yes! Of course. I'll get that right out to you." Reese took the rest of the table's order and came back with their drinks. "So here are your drinks and I will give you all a moment to look over the menu. Also, Mr. West, I told my manager that you were a little hot so she will be adjusting the temp. Sometimes it gets pretty warm in here when there are a lot of bodies.... close to each other." Reese put a lot of emphasis on 'close to each other' causing Tracy to crack his knuckles. *I guess that's my cue to leave,* Reese thought to himself and smirked. "I'll be back in a moment to take your order," Reese informed and left their table. As he was walking towards the kitchen, Thea grabbed his arm and pulled him to the side. Startled, he jumped. "Omigosh, Thea! Don't do that, I almost pissed myself," Reese said, holding his chest exhaling. "Sorry! I didn't mean to scare you," Thea apologized. "It's all good. Tracy is here and clearly he's not too enthused that I am his waiter. I thought you were him trying to harm me," Reese said, shaking his head. "Harm you? Has he threatened you?" Thea asked concerned. "Girl, no! Anyway, what's up?" Reese asked changing the subject. "So I have some tea for you! Can we talk in the back?" Thea asked. Reese looked around to make sure his manager wasn't around and led Thea to the break room. "So what's the tea?" Reese said, taking a seat ready to listen. Thea sat down fast, ready to spill it. "Okay, so I visited that church today. Kingdom Life Ministries. First, let me start off by saying the service was AWESOME. And I will definitely be visiting again real soon. Anyway, to the tea. So after service, Tracy asked for everyone's attention and called his new lady Claudia to the front with him. He pretty much professed his love for her and proposed, honey. And she said YES!" "What!?" Reese asked confused. "I thought they just met or recently started dating," Reese said, disgusted. "Nope! They've been friends for years. He went on and on about how she has been nothing but a great friend, and how happy he is that they decided to take their friendship to another level. He told her that he doesn't need to date her to know that she is the one because God already showed her to him. Baby! He had everyone in there in tears. But, hun-ey, I was just clutching my pearls because I know his other side. He got those folks fooled," Thea informed Reese waiting on his response. "Wooooow….For real?" "Yep!" Thea shook her head as to say yes. "Okay, it's all good," Reese said calmly and got up and paced the room. "So what are you going to do?" Thea asked. Reese stopped pacing and stared his friend straight in the eyes. "Just what I said I would do. I think it's time for me to pay a visit to Kingdom Life Ministries."

Chapter 4

The stars were shining bright, the spring temperature was just right, and jazz music filled the night time air. "This is beautiful!" Claudia said of the candle light dinner Tracy set up for her on his backyard deck. "You're beautiful," Tracy complimented her. "Thank you!" Claudia smiled. Tracy took her by the hand and led her to the middle of the deck. "Can I have this dance?" he asked. "Of course," she answered. Tracy held Claudia close and kissed her neck. "I can't wait to call you my wife," he spoke softly in her ear. She embraced him tighter. "And I can't wait to call you my husband." Tracy pulled back from their embrace and grabbed her hands. "Then we shouldn't wait any longer. Let's get married tonight!" he said excitedly. Claudia was stunned. "Are you serious?" "Yes, let's do it. We can elope," he said, lifting her off her feet. "Elope? Wait a minute. What about premarital counseling and sharing our big day with family and friends?" Claudia said not really feeling the idea of eloping. Tracy placed her back down. "You're right. I just don't want to wait any longer." Claudia put her arms on Tracy's shoulders and clasped her hands behind his neck. "How about this...Tomorrow, we'll call Bishop Goodwin and schedule premarital counseling. Then, in the mean time, we can plan a small intimate wedding. We can be Mr. and Mrs. West in a few weeks. How does that sound?" "That sounds wonderful!" Tracy said, leaning in to kiss her. The sound of loud crash came from up front. "What in the world was that?!" Tracy asked startled by the noise. "Sounds like a wreck. We should go see if everything's okay," Claudia insisted. The two went inside Tracy's house to go investigate. As they were walking inside the living room to exit the front door, they were met with the ringing of Tracy's doorbell. "I hope everything is okay," Tracy said by the urgency of the door bell being continuously pressed. Tracy opened the door and to his dismay, it was Reese. "Reese, what are you doing here?" Reese had been watching Tracy all evening. He planned on trying to talk to Tracy to see if they could somehow give their relationship another chance. However, he knew that conversation wasn't going to happen when he saw Claudia enter Tracy's home. Which angered him tremendously. It angered him so much he decided to crash his car into Tracy's mailbox. Reese was standing at Tracy's doorstep holding his head as if he was in pain, ready to showcase his acting chops. "My God! Are you okay?" Claudia asked. Tracy looked over Reese to see his mailbox smashed.

"Did you hit my mailbox?" Tracy asked not really concerned about Reese. Claudia reached out to Reese. "It looks like you hit your head very hard come inside." An annoyed Tracy shut the door and followed Claudia as she led Reese to the sofa. "What happened?" Claudia asked. "I was on my way to visit a friend nearby when my breaks went out. I lost control of my car and hit your mailbox. I am so sorry, Mr. West," Reese explained. "Do you want to go to the hospital? Claudia asked. "No, it's just a bruise. I am sure I will be fine," Reese answered. "I don't know, it looks pretty bad, you should see a doctor," Claudia insisted. "I am fine. I just wanted to make the owner aware of the damages I caused to the mailbox so I can replace it. I had no idea you were the owner, Mr. West. What a small world," Reese said, still holding his head. "Oh please…" Tracy began ready to call Reese out on all his nonsense. Until he remembered Claudia was there. "Honey, can you get Reese some ice?" Tracy refrained from going off. Reese waited for Claudia to leave before flashing Tracy a huge grin. "So are you happy to see me? I've missed you so much," Reese said, reaching out to Tracy to hug him. Tracy pushed Reese away "Are you crazy? What is wrong with you? Get the hell out of here!" Reese laughed and shook his head. "Wow! Don't act like that. You mean to tell me you are really over all of this?" Reese questioned spinning around to show off his backside in his tight jeans. "Let's be clear. There will never be anything between us. What's done is done. I don't want anything to do with you so just move on. Now leave, so I can get back to having dinner with MY fiancée." "Fiancée, huh? Hmmph!" Reese said, raising his brows. "Yes, my fiancée. So leave now or else I will sue you for damaging my property and file a restraining order on you for stalking me," Tracy warned. "You wouldn't do those things. One, you know suing me is pointless. I am a struggling student, I don't have any money. Two, you have no proof that I am stalking you. All this can be viewed as a coincidence. And, last but not least, you wouldn't take a chance in having your secret exposed." Tracy clenched his fist. "Reese, just go!" he said through his teeth. "Okay! I'll leave under one condition," Reese said. "What?" Tracy grumbled. "I need a new car. A 2016 Lexus LS in red to be exact," Reese said, rubbing his chin. Tracy laughed at Reese's request. "You have got to be out of your rabbit ass mind! I am not buying you shit." "Fine, I am just going to tell your fiancée that—" Reese began before being interrupted by Claudia. "Tell me what?" Claudia asked. Tracy gave Reese an intimidating look. "He was just going to tell you that he didn't need the ice. I am about to walk him out," Tracy answered. "Are you sure?" Claudia asked. "He's fine, dear," Tracy said, not giving Reese a chance to speak. "How are you getting home? You shouldn't be driving without breaks," a concerned Claudia asked. "My friend is on the way to pick me up and I will have my car towed," Reese informed her. "Okay. Well, I thank God that you're alright! I can't say the same about your car, but that's not even important," Claudia said as they walked to the door. "Yeah, I am thankful because it could have been worse. And I am not worried about my car. I am about to get something brand new in a few days," Reese said with a smile, and then winked at Tracy while Claudia wasn't looking. "Praise God! You're so blessed!" Claudia said happily. "Yep, a red 2016 Lexus LS," Reese smiled ear to ear. "Wow!" Claudia said. "Alright, Reese, like I said earlier, don't worry about the mailbox. Accidents happen. Have a good night," Tracy said, rushing Reese out the door. "You have two days," Reese whispered. "Don't forget a red 2016—" Before Reese could finish his sentence, Tracy shut the door in his face. Reese found it amusing. "Oh, Tracy, Tracy, Tracy. You're such a fool. You just don't know what's in store for you."

"Kingdom Life Ministries," Reese said to himself as he pulled up to the church. He found a parking spot. Before getting out of his car, he pulled out his compact mirror to make sure his bruise on his forehead wasn't peeking through the concealer he applied over it. "Perfect as usual," he said, blowing a kiss to himself. He got out of his car and armed the alarm on his brand new red Lexus. Reese took a deep breath and entered the church doors. He was a little early so there was no one in the foyer to greet him. Reese was reading the church mission statement when he heard footsteps. He turned around to see Tracy rushing towards him. "Why are you here?" Tracy said, shoving Reese against the wall. "Whoa whoa whoa! Is this the way guest are treated here?" Reese said with his hands up. "You are not a guest! I did not invite you and you are definitely not welcomed here," Tracy sneered. "Well, I beg to differ. The sign out front says all are welcome," Reese said with a smirk. "I've had enough of this. First, you showed up to my job, and then my home, now my place of worship. I should have handled you when you came to my house!" Tracy said through clenched teeth. "I am just here visiting. I want to experience Kingdom Life Ministries for myself, to see what all the hype is about." "You're not here to visit. You're trying to ruin my life!" Reese sucked his teeth and smiled. "You're right. I am not here to visit. I am here to join! And if you don't keep up with your part of the deal as being my sponsor, everyone here is going to know that you like boys," Reese giggled, and then walked to the sanctuary doors. Before he entered, he turned to Tracy and blew him a kiss. "See you after service, Mr. West." Tracy let out a sound of frustration and punched the wall. Bishop Goodwin and Deacon Roberts entered the foyer to see Tracy pacing and mumbling under his breath. "You alright, brotha?" Deacon Roberts asked. Tracy tried to regain his composure. "It's just been a trying morning. But I am fine," Tracy said, swallowing hard. "Well, let's pray this energy off you because I can't have that trailing behind me," Bishop Goodwin insisted. "Yes, sir," Tracy agreed. "Heavenly Father. Oh, Lord, I call unto You for Tracy. I don't know what's bothering him but I know that You know everything. There is nothing too big or small that You can't handle. So whatever it is that's consuming his mind that's causing great stress, I ask that You remove it now. I ask that You strengthen him and give him the peace that he needs. Clear his mind so that his focus can be on You. Remind him of the word: Cast your cares on the LORD and he will sustain you; he will never let the righteous be shaken. Oh, Father, You are so good! I thank You in advance Lord for putting Your reigning hands in this situation and fixing it, oh God. Yes, God, I thank you! Amen." "Amen. Thank you, Bishop," Tracy said. Bishop Goodwin nodded his head and motioned for Tracy to follow him to his office. Once inside Bishop Goodwin's office, Tracy made himself busy by gathering Bishop's Bible and a few other items he may need during service. Tracy felt Bishop Goodwin watching him. "Is everything okay, sir? Do you need tea or cough drops?" Tracy asked. "No, I am fine. Don't forget to grab my i-Pad and reading glasses," Bishop Goodwin said, still studying Tracy. "Tracy, I bet I know what's bothering you. Is it the stress of planning your wedding?" "No, sir, Claudia has it all worked out. I just have to show up," Tracy laughed lightly. "You're not getting cold feet, are you?" "No, but I hope I can be all she needs and more. I just want to give her the world." "Keep God first in your marriage and he will provide everything you need." Bishop Goodwin smiled and gave Tracy a light pat on his shoulder. Tracy helped Bishop Goodwin put on his clergy robe and followed him to the sanctuary. Praise and Worship Service had already begun. During Praise and Worship service, Bishop Goodwin doesn't like sitting at the pulpit. Instead, he stands amongst the congregation in the front row to praise and worship right along with them. Tracy, too, stood right behind Bishop Goodwin in the second row of pews. Tracy glanced around the full sanctuary, in hopes that Reese left. However, that wasn't the case. Tracy located Reese sitting next to Claudia. Reese caught Tracy's eyes and stared at him with a big smile on his face. Disgusted Tracy rolled his eyes and looked away.

The moment I've been waiting for, Reese thought to himself and chuckled. Altar call. Reese rehearsed in his mind all service of the show he would put on. Now it was time. He slowly made his way up to the altar with a few others. Several ministers were waiting for those who needed prayer. One of the ministers motioned for Reese to come his way. Reese clasped his hands together and rested his chin on them as tears rolled down his cheeks. "Do you have a special prayer request?" the minister asked. "Yes. I need God to heal my broken heart," Reese said, and then burst into more tears. The minister nodded his head and instructed Reese to lift his hands so that he could pray for him. As the minister prayed for Reese. Reese began to sob very loud and rocked side to side. This caught Bishop Goodwin's attention. *Here we go,* Tracy thought as he followed closely behind Bishop Goodwin. Bishop Goodwin stood beside the minister who was praying for Reese. The minister finished up praying and stepped aside as Bishop Goodwin reached for Reese. "Young man, don't let the devil use you. He will lure you into traps that nobody but God will be able to free you from. But if you're not seeking God, you will die in that trap." Reese fell to his knees and continued to sob. "I don't want to live like this anymore. I want to change!" Tracy shook his head at Reese's dramatic display. "If you want to change, then you got to turn away from all that mess that's not of God. The word says: If my people, which are called by my name, shall humble themselves, and pray, and seek my face, and turn from their wicked ways; then will I hear from heaven, and will forgive their sin, and will heal their land. Are you ready to repent?" Bishop Goodwin asked. Reese nodded vehemently. "Yes, sir." "The altar is open. If you came in here messed up and you don't want to leave out the same way, you need to get up here." Bishop Goodwin extended an invitation once more. Reese continued to kneel at the altar pretending to repent for his sins. Once he was done, he stood up and wiped his tears with a tissue that was given to him by an altar worker. Not too longer afterwards, Bishop Goodwin was announcing to the congregation that not only did Reese want to be baptized but wanted to join the church as well. The congregation clapped and cheered at the announcement. One by one, the members of the church welcomed Reese with a hug. "Praise God! Welcome to the family, Reese!" Claudia said excitedly as she hugged him. As the two embraced, Reese glanced at Tracy who was staring at him cold-heartedly. Reese, unbothered by Tracy, winked at him and smiled.

Chapter 5

A couple weeks have gone by since Reese last stepped his foot inside Kingdom Life Ministries. Several members reached out to him showing concern about his whereabouts. He blamed his absence on not being able to get an off day from work on Sundays. But in reality, he actually felt convicted from standing in front of all those people playing with God. Reese has every intention of righting his wrongs but it was one last thing he needed to do before really turning over a new leaf. After all the plotting and waiting, Reese felt today would be the perfect occasion to expose Tracy. The parking lot at Kingdom Life Ministries was full to capacity. "Full house I see," Reese said to himself with a smirk. He walked inside the church wearing a bright pink suit which got him many looks and whispers. The reaction he was going for. He sat on the very last pew in the sanctuary. Soft music played as the mothers of the bride and groom entered the sanctuary. They lit the candelabras and were led to their seats. Bishop Goodwin and Tracy walked to the front of the church and stood at the altar. Reese watched with everyone else the processional of Tracy and Claudia's wedding ceremony. Everyone stood as Claudia made her way down the aisle. She looked so happy and beautiful as her father stood next to her to give her hand to Tracy. Reese began to have second thoughts on his plan but once he looked at Tracy cheesing from ear to ear, it made him nauseous. *You won't be smiling for too long*, Reese thought. Bishop Goodwin began the ceremony with opening remarks followed by prayer. Reese yawned at the lengthiness of the prayer. But he perked up once the exchanging of vows began. Bishop Goodwin handed Tracy a microphone. Tracy faced Claudia and held her hand. "Claudia, I would have never thought in a million years that we would be standing here getting married. For so long you have been nothing but an awesome friend. You have always been there to encourage and motivate me. You've prayed with me and prayed for me at times when I couldn't pray for myself. You're such an amazing beautiful woman. I am so thankful that God placed you in my life. I promise that I will stand with you, walk with you, carry you, encourage you, laugh with you, cry with you, grow with you; I will love you forever and do everything in my power to keep you happy until the end of time." Tracy's eyes welled up with tears as he spoke to an also teary eyed Claudia. Reese rolled his eyes at the mushiness of it all. "Sick of this…" Reese whispered and stood up to walk into the aisle. As he walked up the aisle towards the altar he clapped loudly and slowly. Everyone in the sanctuary stared at Reese shocked and confused. "Reese, what are you doing?" Claudia asked while still keeping a smile on her face. Tracy looked as if he seen a ghost as he stood speechless. "Sooo you're really going to do this? You're really going to marry this woman and lie in front of all these people? You were just in relationship with me a month ago! Tell them how you made love to me! Over and over again!" Reese said loudly so everyone could hear. "Yeah, you all heard right, I was his boyfriend and he took very good care of me. Monetary and sexually," Reese said with a big smile on his face. "Well, Lord, I done heard it all." "Omigod!" "What?" "Wow!" "This is crazy!" "Oooh child." "I always said he looked a little suspect." The sanctuary air was filled with gasp and chatter. Claudia looked at Tracy with disgust and let go of his hand. "Tracy, is this true?" she asked. "Yes, ma'am it's true," Reese chimed in. "I didn't ask you!" Claudia yelled at Reese. "Well, bitch, I'm telling you!" Reese yelled back. Tracy full of rage tackled Reese down to the floor like a linebacker and punched him repeatedly. This caused an uproar in the church. It took Bishop Goodwin, Deacon Roberts, and few others to get Tracy off Reese. "Stop, Tracy! You're going to kill him!"

Bishop Goodwin warned. "I want him dead! Let me kill him!" Tracy said, charging back at Reese. "No, he's not worth it," Deacon Roberts said, pulling Tracy back. Bishop Goodwin silenced the sanctuary and made sure that a distraught Claudia was alright. She was sitting in between her mother and First Lady Valerie sobbing. "You happy now?" Tracy asked Reese out of breath. "This is what you wanted, right? To humiliate and expose me. So now that you've done it, you can move on with your life! Yes, everybody, it's true. I had relations with him. I am not proud of what I did, I led him on for my own selfish reasons. I didn't want to continue on with him or that lifestyle, period. So, for weeks now, he has been making my life hell. I am so sorry, Claudia, that you had to find out this way. Bishop, First Lady, friends, family, Kingdom Life Ministries, I hope you all can find it in your hearts to forgive me." A few brothers helped Reese to his feet and escorted him out the church. First Lady Valerie led a still distraught Claudia to her office along with Claudia's mother. Tracy shook his head full of remorse as he watched Claudia leave the sanctuary. "Guests and members, as you can see, the ceremony will not continue on. I am deeply grieved by what transpired here today. I ask that you all don't let this be the talk of the town. Gossiping and judging will not help this situation. I ask that you pray for all those involved. With that being said, you all are dismissed. Govern yourselves accordingly!" Bishop Goodwin announced and left the sanctuary to go his office. Deacon Roberts followed close behind him. "Pastor, man, did you have any idea that Tracy is gay?" Deacon Roberts asked as they entered the office. "No, I didn't know," Bishop Goodwin said, taking a seat at his desk. "Wow, I am astonished by your lack of discernment when it came to this," Deacon Roberts said, taking a seat as well. Bishop Goodwin raised his eyebrows showing disapproval. "I mean you see through everything. God shows you so much. I'm just sayin'." Deacon Roberts said, cleaning up his previous statement. "Well, that wasn't shown to me. Besides, you didn't know either." "True. But I knew that Reese was a sissy from the jump!" Deacon Roberts snickered. "That enough, Deac," Bishop Goodwin said as he rubbed his temples. There was a knock at the door. "Come in!" Bishop Goodwin answered the knock. Tracy walked inside looking somber. "Can we talk?" Tracy asked. "Sure. Deacon Roberts, can you go see if everyone has left the sanctuary?" Bishop Goodwin spoke. "Yes, sir. Tracy, brotha, I am so sorry things went down the way it did. I know that had to be embarrassing. Getting exposed by your gay lover. I mean this is the type of stuff that happens on T.V. But this real life just happened. I know we go laugh about this one day." Bishop Goodwin scrunched up his face at Deacon Roberts. "Deac, sanctuary. Thank you," Bishop Goodwin said, pointing to the door for him to leave. "Sorry. Too soon? I'm a go to the sanctuary now," Deacon Roberts said awkwardly before leaving the office. "Deacon Roberts, he doesn't have a filter, but you got to love him," Bishop Goodwin said, trying to lightening things up. "That's true." Tracy said, forcing a half smile. "Bishop, if you want me to leave the church, I will." "Leave the church?" "Yes, sir. I know this had to be just as embarrassing to you as it was for me. I can barely face you right now and I don't think I will be able to face the church again." "I don't want you to leave this ministry." "But don't you hate homosexuals?" "No! I hate the sin not the people." "Bishop, but how do you feel about me? I am not gay. I don't have desires for men. Reese was the only one I had relations with and I deeply regret it." "Am I shocked by your actions? Yes! However, I still love you and I want to continue to cover you. If I turned away everyone with issues of immorality, I would have an empty church. We all have issues of the flesh. That's why we are here! Because God can fix it. I am not your judge, so you don't have to explain or prove to me anything on this matter. Turn it all over to God. Repent, recommit, and recover."

Tracy nodded his head in agreement with Bishop Goodwin's instructions. He took a deep breath and spoke. "My role as armor bearer—"

"For the time being, I am going to relieve you of your duties as my armor bearer. I need to seek the Lord's guidance on if this will be temporary or permanently. Bishop Goodwin said before Tracy could finish. "Yes, sir, I understand." Bishop Goodwin ended their discussion with prayer, praying that God forgives and repairs the damage that affected all that was involved. He also thanked God for freeing Tracy from the bondage he was in. Tracy left Bishop Goodwin's office feeling like a huge weight was lifted off his shoulders. He knew a lot of damage control was in order but he was ready to face it head on.

A month has passed since the "what's done in the dark always come to light shining" moment. It took everything in Tracy to keep attending Kingdom Life Ministries. He saw the looks and heard the whispers that followed after the incident. The awkward short conversations with members often made him not want to socialize after service. In spite of it all, he has kept pressing and praying and now things seem to be getting back to normal in his life. He walked into the foyer to see Claudia standing there speaking with an usher. They've only spoken a few times and briefly since the situation. Claudia went on a short vacation to what was supposed to be their honeymoon to regroup. Now she was back and surprisingly she greeted Tracy with a big smile. "Hi, Claudia. How are you?" Tracy asked. "I am well, and you?" "I am doing a lot better." "That's good to know." "You're glowing. You look very refreshed and beautiful as always," Tracy complimented. "Thank you! That's what beach life will do for you." "Uh-oh! You didn't go to the beach and get your groove back, did you?" Tracy let out a small laugh. "Hey, now watch it!" Claudia smiled and playfully shoved him. Tracy opened the sanctuary door for Claudia to enter. Once inside the sanctuary, he took a seat and to his surprise, Claudia came and sat next to him. "We're still friends, right?" Tracy asked. "For life," Claudia answered. They gave each other a fist bump and exchanged smiles.

Finally ready to right his wrongs, Reese entered the church foyer. An usher immediately stopped him before he could go inside the sanctuary. "Now I know the sign out front says all are welcome, but if you're here to start drama, you need to leave." "No, ma'am, I am not here for that," Reese informed. "Then why are you here?" the usher said with a little attitude. "The same reason you are here," Reese said, trying not to match her tone. Deacon Roberts noticed Reese from the sanctuary and came out to the foyer. "Is there problem?" Deacon Roberts asked. "No, sir, I just want to come to service. To pray, praise, worship, and get a word. Is that okay?" Reese responded. Bishop Goodwin stood at the pulpit. "Let him in." Everyone turned to the sanctuary doors as Reese walked in. Reese walked to the altar. Deacon Roberts stood nearby just in case Reese wanted to act a fool. "Bishop Goodwin, I am so sorry for the way that I behaved," Reese began, and then turned to face the congregation. "I also want to apologize to everyone here. Claudia, I am so sorry for ruining your beautiful day. Tracy, I am sorry for blackmailing you and shaking up your life. I was miserable and went about everything the wrong way. I was functioning from a place of hurt that was build up over many years. Tracy is just the one I decided to take it all out on. I hope you all can forgive me as I seek the Lord's forgiveness." The whole church prayed as Reese   laid prostrate on the altar in repentance. "The word says: For if ye forgive men their trespasses, your heavenly Father will also forgive you. Let us have a heart to forgive and forget like our Savior," Bishop Goodwin spoke. Many others joined Reese at the altar, two of them being Tracy and Claudia.

The Sermon

Bishop Goodwin stood up at the pulpit after an atmosphere changing praise and worship service. He looked at the congregation as many of them continued to clap, quicken, and praise God. "Give God some praise in this place. Bless his name. For he is worthy! We owe him all the glory! I am so happy to be standing here. Somebody didn't get to stand up this morning. So even when I don't feel like it, I'm going to give God what I owe him. Amen." The congregation clapped and yelled out Hallelujah. Bishop Goodwin set his Bible and i-pad on his podium. He pushed them to the side for he won't be using them today. "Well, saints, I wish I could tell you all that I have a message prepared for you. But I don't. So I am asking you all to pray that God has his way." Bishop Goodwin led the congregation in prayer and asked them to be seated. "As I look out at all of your faces, some old and some new, I am blessed with your presence. When I and Valerie started this ministry, I never guessed it would've grown as fast as it has. But I am truly thankful for each and every last one of you and for the future saints God adds. Kingdom Life Ministries, as you all know, over the last few months, our church has been tried and tested.

Our members have gone through so much. From fighting amongst each other, to fighting with ourselves, and going countless rounds with the enemy. So today I want to remind some of you all of why we are here. This church is not for perfect people. Yes, we serve a perfect God and we strive to be like him. But we have flaws. So next time you judge someone because they're still a baby in Christ who is not on the spirituality level as yourself, think about the time when you were a baby in Christ. Yes, I am about to step on some toes, but do know this is coming from a place of love. I want everyone here and everyone who ever walks in these doors to feel free, welcomed, and loved. That woman that you claimed to hate so much, she was raped continuously as a kid. She had to grow up fast. Yet, you tear her down because of past decisions she's made that she has learned from and moved past. She came here to be healed. Why would you stand in the way of her breakthrough? Then we have saints who laugh at someone because of their sexual preference. Don't you know God is a deliverer? Yet, we have some who don't want to invite those type here. So it seems we have saints who pick and choose which sin they are okay with. When some of you had children out of wedlock, some of you are still fornicating, cussing like sailors, smoking, drinking, lying, stealing, cheating, backbiting and just doing the most. Just imagine if God exposed your dirt. Some of you need to be praising him for not exposing you! So, if you have issues of immorality past or present that God didn't expose, why is it okay for you to expose others'? You don't have the right! Let's not be those judgmental saints who run people out of the church, and then go out into the world and keep up more hell than the unsaved. Examine yourself and realize this church is our hospital, this is our place of worship, our place of fellowship, we can transform and grow spiritually here. So next time someone walks in these doors messed up and going through, remember that God can turn their mess into a message." Bishop Goodwin wrapped up his sermon and extended an invitation for altar call. Half the congregation went up for prayer. Many repenting, two being baptized, and three joined the church. This new fresh fire caused Kingdom Life Ministries to rejoice and celebrate. The service ended with everyone hugging one another.

***

First Lady Valerie headed back to Bishop Goodwin's office after the commotion in the sanctuary. After service, one of the members felt very ill and passed out. After corporate prayer and tending to the member, she felt better. Lady Valerie's attention was drawn to her husband's desk. "What is that?" she said to herself as she walked closer to view the object. It was a pregnancy test. She picked it up with a napkin. The test read positive. "Hey, honey, let's get out of here," Bishop Goodwin said, walking into his office. Lady Valerie didn't look up at him. "What's that?" Bishop Goodwin walked closer to her. Lady Valerie looked at her husband baffled. "It's a pregnancy test?" she handed it to him. Shocked, Bishop Goodwin's eyes got big at the positive sign. "Honey! Are you pregnant?" His shock turned into joy. Lady Valerie stared at him blankly. "No, I am not pregnant. That is not my test." "Well, who does it belong to?" he asked confused. "It's mine" the two heard a voice say. They turned to see Tara standing at the door. "The test is mine. I am pregnant."

COMING SOON

Scandals in the Sanctuary II: The

Altar is Open

About the Author

SC Hill is a passionate Fiction Author & Entrepreneur who writes and resides in Nashville, Tennessee. Hailing from the same area, her passion for writing began early on and it has stayed with her ever since.

When she isn't creating, SC Hill still enjoys to nurture her creative side with cooking, drawing, and painting. She also has an avid interest in fitness and music and loves going to church. Most importantly, SC Hill likes spending quality time with her wonderful family. She is happily married and is the proud mother of three children.

Currently, SC Hill is continuing to write her "Scandals in the Sanctuary" series and is studying at Lipscomb University. As a healthy foodie, she is also putting together a recipe book to prove that eating healthy doesn't have to mean eating bland.

To find out more about SC Hill and her upcoming books, visit: **dreamersvisionpub.com**

www.ingramcontent.com/pod-product-compliance
Lightning Source LLC
Chambersburg PA
CBHW031403250626
47155CB00004B/1390